THE DIVAS: VERONIQUE

Other books in *The Divas* series
by Victoria Christopher Murray

India
Diamond

THE DIVAS: VERONIQUE

Victoria Christopher Murray

POCKET BOOKS

New York   London   Toronto   Sydney

Pocket Books
A Division of Simon & Schuster, Inc.
1230 Avenue of the Americas
New York, NY 10020

First Pocket Books trade paperback edition March 2009

POCKET and colophon are registered trademarks of Simon & Schuster, Inc.

For information about special discounts for bulk purchases,
please contact Simon & Schuster Special Sales at 1-800-456-6798
or business@simonandschuster.com.

Designed by Jamie Kerner

Manufactured in the United States of America

10 9 8 7 6 5 4 3 2 1

Library of Congress Cataloging-in-Publication Data is available.

ISBN-13: 978-1-4165-6350-1
ISBN-10:   1-4165-6350-4

THE DIVAS: VERONIQUE

Chapter One

My whole life is over!

I know I sound all over-the-top dramatic like my girl Diamond, but I can't help it. I'm still walking around in a crazy funk because everything I've dreamed about all my life is now . . . so . . . over.

It's been more than a week and I still can't believe it. We lost! The Divine Divas lost the Glory 2 God talent contest in San Francisco. Can you even believe it? I don't know if we came in second or third or last. It doesn't even matter—we didn't come in first, and that means that we aren't going to be getting on any kind of airplane going anywhere near the NYC.

New York—that was my real dream. Everyone thought that I just wanted to be a star. Well, duh! I mean, for real—who wouldn't want to get a phat contract and cut lots of tracks? That $250,000 recording deal sounded real good to me, 'cause then I would've been able to help my mama move me and my brothers out of this run-down apartment building. But even though I was feelin' the bucks, what I wanted more than the Benjamins was that trip to New York.

And that had been all part of my plan.

Last week at this time, Diamond, Aaliyah, and I were flying to San Francisco. And then, later on, we hooked up with India. We were supposed to get on that stage with guns blazing and smoke the competition.

But it didn't happen.

Just thinking about how we lost gave me a headache. I guess that was why it took me forever to walk home from the bus stop, and longer than forever to walk up the stairs to the third floor. I guess losing just made you tired.

Reaching for something in the distance
So close you can almost taste it . . .

I snatched the plugs from my MP3 player out of my ears and turned off my all-time favorite song. Natasha Bedingfield may have been the one blowin', but her words were all about me. With the Divine Divas, I was so close, but now it was all so far away.

I took my key out of my pocket. And then the moment I put it in the lock, every single solitary thought I had about the Divine Divas, New York, and Natasha left my mind. My apartment door swung open, and I'm telling you, I was scared straight. No one was supposed to be here. Mama was still at work. And D'Andre, D'Angelo, D'Marcus, and D'Wight were still with our grandmother. Big Mama never brought them home until around six. So I just knew there was some kind of burglar in our house.

But then I saw who it was and I wasn't scared anymore. I was just mad.

"Well, well, well!" D'Wayne grinned at me with a toothpick stuck in between his two big buck front teeth. "If it isn't the star herself. How ya doing, Lil' Mama?"

"My name is Veronique," I growled at him.

"Don't you think I know what your name is?" He was looking at me with his eyes all wide. It made me want to barf—all over him. "But I like calling you Lil' Mama."

I didn't care what he liked calling me. All I wanted to know was what he was doing in my house. "Why are you here?" Even though it wasn't all that warm outside, I stayed in the hallway, not wanting to step one foot into my own apartment—not as long as D'Wayne was there.

"Who do you think you are asking me that?" His grin was all the way gone, and he screwed up his face like he was eating something nasty. "You're not grown. What would your mama say?"

I hoped my mama would say that he needed to get up out of our house. But I had a bad feeling that she wouldn't say that. Mama was probably the reason why big-tooth D'Wayne was in our apartment.

"I don't need to be answering your questions," he said as I slowly walked past him. "You don't pay no bills around here." D'Wayne closed the door and just had to add, "But if you need to know something, it's that I'm gonna be here a lot from now on. Your mama and I are back together."

I rolled my eyes, but I didn't let D'Wayne see me. And he didn't hear the voice in my head either. The voice that said he was nothing but a lying fool.

He followed me into the kitchen and kept right on talking. "Your mama and I are getting married."

Yeah, right, I talked inside my head again. I wasn't even a little bit worried. D'Wayne was always saying that. Ever since

I was about six or seven years old, he'd come around and tell Mama he wanted to get married. Sometimes he would stay with us for a long time. But then it always went down the same way—one day I'd wake up and he'd be gone. And Mama would be crying. And then not too long after that, Mama would have a baby.

I might be only fifteen years old, but I peeped D'Wayne a long time ago. The thing was, I couldn't figure out why my mom hadn't. I just hoped that this time, my mama didn't end up having another baby. Not that I didn't love my little brothers to Reese's pieces, but four knuckleheads were way more than enough for me.

"So now that I'm gonna marry your mama . . ."

Dude, why are you still talking to me?

"I'm gonna be your daddy!"

I stopped all that talking inside my head and turned around so fast I almost fell over. "You will never be my daddy!" I screamed.

I ran straight to my bedroom and slammed the door. I knew that if my mother was home, she'd come after me for dissin' D'Wayne like that, but I didn't care. I threw my backpack on the floor so hard it felt like my whole room shook.

How could he say something so stupid to me? That man made me crazy-sick. He would never be my daddy. I already had a father, and I didn't need a broke-down one like D'Wayne.

I bounced so hard on my bed that the legs wobbled like the whole thing was about to fall apart. That would've been some mad mess. If I broke this bed, my mother would have a fit. So I backed up a bit, closed my eyes, and tried not to think about that man outside my room.

Instead, I thought about another man, a really handsome one. With a bald head and a little bit of a beard.

Of course the man was tall, like Diamond's father. He had smooth, Hershey chocolate–colored skin, like Aaliyah's father. And he had lots of muscles, like India's father. He was strong, and he could whip D'Wayne's big ole butt any time he wanted.

I laughed out loud just thinking about my daddy beating down D'Wayne, but I didn't laugh for long. Thinking about my father always made me feel happy and sad at the same time.

Pushing up off the bed, I sat at my keyboard. Even though I tried to make up a new song every day, today I didn't feel like playing a thing.

I stood and pressed my nose against the tiny window. It was hard to see anything through the dirt from the outside that made the glass always so murky, but I could see clear down into the alley. Since the garbage had been picked up this morning, the alleyway was empty. No cats or rats or addicts hunting for their dinner through the trash. And right now, it didn't stink like it always did. It might have been fine now, but by tomorrow, everything would be back to ghetto-normal.

I bounced on my bed, lay down, and closed my eyes. I went right back to thinking about my daddy—and him coming to take me away from this crazy mess. In my head, I could almost see my father—even though I couldn't remember ever seeing him in person. All I had were those old, faded-out pictures hanging on my wall of my mother and father back in the day.

But I had the best picture of my father in my mind. Just like Diamond looked like her dad, I was sure I looked just like mine.

I knew for sure what my dad sounded like. And what he would say to me the first time he saw me. *"Baby girl, I've been looking for you forever. But now that you found me, I promise we'll always be together."* And then he would hug me for a long time, before he said something awesome like, *"I love you."*

I just had to find a way to get to my dad now that the Divine Diva plan was a bust. I had to find a way to get to New York—and when I got there, I would find my daddy. Trust and know.

Chapter Two

Right in the middle of this great dream I was having about my dad coming home, I heard a whole lotta knocking in my head. And then, I opened my eyes. That wasn't coming from the inside—it was all from the outside.

I shot up out of my bed, but before I opened my bedroom door, I leaned against the wood and listened—just to make sure this wasn't some kind of trick by D'Wayne.

"Special! Open this door!"

When I heard Big Mama calling, I ran through the living room, jumping over a bunch of yellow and red Tonka trucks like I was the star of the track team. I didn't have a clue how long my grandmother had been standing out there, but I could tell by the way she was yelling and banging that she was crazy-mad.

"What took you so long, Special?" my grandmother asked, calling me by the name that she'd made up for me when I was a little girl. She pushed my baby brother, D'Wight, into my arms and then stomped inside. "I couldn't find my key!"

I rested D'Wight on my hip, but before I could even turn around, D'Andre, one of the twins, almost knocked me down.

"Hey!" I yelled.

Then, D'Angelo, the other twin, and D'Marcus tried to run me over, too.

"You need to get out the way," D'Andre screamed before he slammed the door to their bedroom.

I looked at my grandmother, waiting for her to say something to those knuckleheads. But she was already leaning back on the couch and grabbing a cigarette from her purse.

I shook my head. I couldn't stand eight-year-old boys—or six-year-old boys. But there was not a thing I could do, since they were my brothers.

D'Wight giggled when I dumped him on the couch and let him bounce like a big ole ball. He kicked his legs as I unzipped his jacket.

"Stop it!" I said. Sometimes, I couldn't stand one-year-old boys either. But when D'Wight looked at me with his big, round eyes, I couldn't be mad anymore. He still liked me and didn't talk back the way D'Andre and 'em did.

"How ya doin'?" I asked my brother in that baby-talk, baby-voice.

"Would you stop talkin' to him like that?" my grandmother kinda growled. "All y'all are always talkin' to him like he's a baby."

In my head, I rolled my eyes. D'Wight *was* a baby, but I didn't say a single, solitary word. My friends called my mother the Queen of Mean, but where do they think she got all of that mean stuff from—Big Mama! My grandmother would give me a left-handed back slap in a minute.

So I just smiled and said, "Yes, ma'am."

Then Big Mama smiled, too. "What took you so long to answer the door?" she asked me as she puffed on her cigarette.

I waved the smoke out of my and D'Wight's face. But she didn't care. Big Mama took another toke, then blew more smoke like she was aiming for me.

"I was in my room," I said and coughed at the same time. "I thought D'Wayne was going to answer the door."

That made Big Mama put down her cigarette. She stared at me as if I'd just given her some crazy-bad news. I guess saying D'Wayne's name was about as crazy as it could get.

"D'Wayne?" Big Mama asked.

I could tell by the look on her face—like she was tasting and smelling and hearing something nasty—that she knew who I was talking about.

I nodded my head over and over like I wanted to make sure Big Mama really got it. Inside, I was grinning. It was gonna be on now! Trust and know. Big Mama was gonna do something.

My grandmother put out her cigarette even though she wasn't close to being finished. That was a good sign. She was mad!

She took D'Wight from my lap. "Did you finish your homework?"

I frowned. That was it? My grandmother was supposed to be standing up, whooping and hollering. She was supposed to say that I didn't have a thing to worry about because as long as she was my grandmother, D'Wayne was going to have to go. But she didn't say any of that. I didn't get it.

"I don't have any homework; today's Friday and they never give homework on the weekend."

Big Mama rolled her eyes. "That school cost so much, they need to be giving homework every day." She put D'Wight on the floor and let him play around with those trucks that were all over the place.

"Don't worry, Big Mama. They give us a lot. I have a couple

of reports I have to turn in next week. I'm working really hard this year."

That seemed to make my grandmother happier.

"So, you're still doing good? Keeping your grades up?"

This was one of those everyday questions. Every day when she brought my brothers home, Big Mama asked me how I was doing in school. "Yes, ma'am," I said just like I always did.

"And how're you and the girls doing? Since you lost that contest?"

That was a new question. In the week since we'd lost, Big Mama hadn't said a single solitary thing about the Divine Divas. And I was glad, 'cause there was not much I wanted to say about that, either.

At first, I didn't answer. Just reached for the remote and turned on the television. D'Wight clapped his hands when Tom and Jerry ran across the screen.

Finally I said, "Big Mama, I can't believe we lost. I wanted that contract so bad so that I wouldn't have to be here any-more." I spread my arms open wide so that my grandmother would know that I was talking about this pitiful living room with the faded mint-green walls and the mud-brown tweed couch and matching love seat that were as old as I was. And the pine coffee and end tables with all those scratches and chipped edges. And the ugly green, brown, and yellow rug in the middle of the living room that was unraveling at both ends. "I hate living here," I said. "The Divine Divas was sup-posed to be my way out."

Big Mama raised her eyebrows. "And where were you going to go with your fifteen-year-old self?"

"Not just me, Big Mama. I wanted to buy a house for Mama. A big house," I scooted closer to my grandmother, "so that you could live with us, too."

While D'Wight cracked up at something that Tom was doing to Jerry on TV, my grandma put her arms around me.

"That singing thing was nice, but it's not your ticket, baby. That school, your education, that's your way out."

I rested my head on Big Mama's shoulder.

Big Mama kept on talking. "Why do you think God made it so you could go to that expensive school?"

"The only reason I'm there is because of the scholarship and Mr. Linden."

That was the real deal—Diamond's father got me into Holy Cross Prep. He was on the board, and even though there was a whole long waiting list, my name got bumped right to the top.

"That's what I'm talking about," Big Mama said. "Who do you think put all of that in motion? It was the Lord, Special. God made it so that you could go to that school."

"On scholarship." I meant to say that under my breath, but Big Mama heard me and made me sit up straight. She shook her finger at me, and all the wooden bangles on her arm clanked together like they were singing a song.

"A scholarship is nothing to be ashamed of, young lady. It's an honor. People recognized how special you are and wanted to give you a chance. Do you know how many girls would love to have your life?"

I was getting ready to laugh, but I didn't because Big Mama looked serious. Who in the whole wide world would want my life? Now, my sistah Diamond—she was living fab and large for real. Even India and Aaliyah had it going on. But me? Please! Who would want to live in a teeny, tiny apartment in Compton with four little brats and their mother?

"You might not think you have anything," Big Mama said, like she could read my mind. "But there're girls who are never going to have the opportunities you have. How many girls in this neighborhood are going to a fancy school like yours?"

I shrugged. I didn't know a lot of girls on this block. There used to be a lot of Black kids who lived here, but now mostly everybody spoke Spanish. And anyway, it wasn't like I hung out here. I've been going to Holy Cross Prep since the third grade. Ever since my mother took me to Hope Chapel and we met Pastor Ford and I met Diamond, India, and Aaliyah.

"God has a great future planned for you, Special. Just remember that; remember Jeremiah twenty-nine eleven." Big Mama gave me an extra hug. "You know I'm proud of you, right?"

"Yeah," I mumbled.

Big Mama wasn't having it. "You'd better move your lips when you talk, girl." She stood up, and even though she put her hands on her hips, I could tell she wasn't all the way mad. "That's not the way my granddaughter, the future lawyer, is supposed to be talking."

"I thought you wanted me to be a doctor."

She sat back down next to me and patted my head. But I could hardly feel it through all of my hair. "That was last week. Now, are you going to hold your head up high and learn a lot so that you can give me some free lawyer advice?"

I laughed. Last week when my grandmother wanted me to be a doctor, she wanted free annual checkups. "Yes, ma'am," I said, and tapped her head just like she'd done to mine. I loved my grandmother's hair—that's why I wore mine exactly the same way—in a big ole wild curly-twisty 'fro.

"That's better." Big Mama looked straight into my eyes. "You know we're all counting on you."

"I know." I tried not to sigh.

Big Mama was back to her everyday talk. This was something she always said. And what she would say next was something she always asked. "You're gonna do it, right, Special?"

"Yes, ma'am."

"You're gonna be the first girl-child in this family to break the cycle."

"Yes, ma'am."

"You're not gonna have a baby before your time, are you?"

"No, ma'am."

"It's up to you, Special." Big Mama hugged me, as if that was the prize for getting all the answers right. "Break the curse."

I hugged my grandmother back, just like I did every day. I never could figure out why she said the same thing to me over and over. I guess she figured the more she said it, the more I would hear it. And the more I heard it, the more I would do it.

Well, Big Mama didn't have a single, solitary thing to worry about. I wasn't about to mess up and be stuck in this kind of life. I looked around the living room again.

Trust and know, I was gonna break the cycle, break the curse, break whatever. I was not going to end up living any kind of life like my mother's.

Chapter Three

This had to be one of the worst days of my life.

First, I had to stay in and watch my brothers while Diamond, India, and even Aaliyah hung together at the Beverly Center. And it wasn't even like my mom was working. When I asked her this morning if I could hang with my sistahs, she said, "You can't, baby. I need to do something with D'Wayne." And then she grinned at him, while he sat at the kitchen table with all of my brothers, laughing and talking and eating up all the food.

"You don't have to go to work?" I asked.

I don't know if it was the way I said that or if it was the way I was trying to stare down D'Wayne. But whatever, Mama didn't like it.

"Who do you think you are asking me that?"

I didn't know why my mother went off. She was acting just like the name Diamond had given her—the Queen of Mean. "What, Mama? I just wanted to know if you had to work."

"You don't need to be asking me nothin' like that. I'm the

only one paying bills around here, and I'm the only one who needs to be asking questions."

My mama always sang that same ole sorry song about working hard and paying bills. Most of the time, I didn't even trip. But then I looked at D'Wayne gobbling down the waffles, and that made me crazy-mad.

"You need to stay here and help out a little bit," my mother said. Her voice was softer now. "Watch your brothers for me. When we get back, you can catch up with your friends."

"Yes, Mama."

I turned to walk right out of that kitchen.

"Where're you going?" she asked. "You don't want no breakfast?"

"No, ma'am," I said just before I closed my bedroom door.

This wasn't the first time I had to babysit my brothers on a Saturday. It just got to me today because D'Wayne was here.

So while my Mama was out with D'Wayne and my sistahs were hanging at the Beverly Center, I spent the whole day breaking up fights between D'Andre and D'Angelo, helping D'Marcus with his science project, changing D'Wight's pull-ups, making all of them peanut butter and jelly sandwiches, cleaning up their mess and a million other things that I didn't want to do.

It wasn't until about eight o'clock when Mama and D'Wayne finally came home—with a whole bunch of stuff. About five Mexican guys came walking through the door carrying all kinds of things—a new couch, three tables, two lamps. Even a new rug.

And there were two more guys behind them carrying one of those flat-screen TVs. I was wondering, though, why it didn't come in a box.

"Look what D'Wayne got us." Mama was beaming like it was Christmas.

My brothers were hanging on D'Wayne while he gave those Mexican guys all of our old stuff—except for the old TV. When he told those guys to carry that into my brothers' bedroom, D'Andre and 'em lost their minds. They were cheering like they'd gotten a whole week off from school or something.

"You see all this, Vee?" Mama asked, sounding so happy as she straightened out the new rug.

All I did was nod. I wasn't even trying to act like I was excited. I mean, yeah, who wouldn't want to have some new furniture?

But I knew the real deal. Every single solitary time D'Wayne came back, he did this. Last time, he bought Mama a new car. And the time before that, we ended up with a new refrigerator and microwave in the kitchen.

That was the thing I think Mama liked best about D'Wayne—he always came back with his pockets full of dollars. And truth—even when he was gone, he sent money for D'Andre and 'em. I thought he was a fool, but I had to give him props for at least doing that, even though the money never helped the broken heart he always left Mama with.

Everyone was laughing and having a good time, but after I watched for a little while, I just went back into my room. None of them would miss me, but that was okay. I could be by myself in peace, sit at my keyboard and jam.

I'd just gotten the sheet music for my favorite song and was already rockin' "Unwritten" like I was hanging out with Natasha's band.

When I heard the knock on my bedroom door, I pretended like I didn't hear a thing. It had to be my mother (because my brothers hardly ever knocked), and I knew all she wanted was for me to see all the stuff D'Wayne bought.

I grabbed my headphones and covered my ears right before my mother came into my room.

"Vee, don't you hear me calling you?"

"Huh?" I said, trying to fake it. My eyes were all wide, like I was surprised. "Oh, Mama." I pulled my headphones off. "Did you say something?"

My mother twisted her lips in that way that let me know she knew what was up. "I *said* you have a call." She waved the phone at me. "It's Pastor Ford."

I jumped right out of my chair. "Thanks, Mama." I grabbed the cordless phone before I said, "Hey, Pastor," as I was closing my door. That was the only way I was going to hear, because D'Wayne had that new TV on blast.

"How are you, Veronique?"

"Fine."

"Great, listen, are you free to come to my house tomorrow evening? I want to have a little celebration for you and the other Divine Divas."

Now, this was crazy-weird. What was wrong with Pastor? Did she forget that we'd lost? "But we didn't win," I said, because obviously she needed to be reminded.

"I told you ladies before, you're winners to me. And you're winners in God's eyes. We need to celebrate all that you did accomplish."

For the first time since losing, I felt like a winner. That was the great thing about our pastor. She was crazy-cool when it came to making other people feel good.

"We're going to get together around four. That'll give me a couple of hours after the second service ends."

"That's fine," I said, feeling better than I had all day. I loved going to Pastor's. She lived in this big ole house on the hill—it was even bigger than the house Diamond lived in. It looked like a mansion to me. "Can my mom come, too?"

"Definitely. I didn't mention it to her, I wanted to talk to the Diva first."

She laughed, and I laughed with her. "Okay, Pastor. We'll be there."

This was gonna be great. Dinner at Pastor's, just me and my mom. For a little while, my mom could concentrate on me.

I yelled, "Mama," before I had even opened up my door. I was grinning until I got to the living room. My mom was hugged up on the new couch with D'Wayne. And D'Andre and 'em were all stretched out on the floor. Every single one of them was staring at the flat-screen TV.

I closed my eyes and made a wish, but when I opened them, D'Wayne was still there. Maybe I shouldn't have made a wish. Maybe I should've said a prayer.

"Mama," I said, stepping over all of D'Wight's toys, "Pastor Ford invited us to her house tomorrow after second service. You want me to call Big Mama so she can watch D'Andre and 'em?"

"Ah, Vee, I can't go. I gotta work. I can't miss two days in a row."

"But, Mama, Pastor wants to have a celebration for the Divine Divas because she said we were winners no matter what happened."

My mother gave me a loud sigh, like I was getting on her nerves. "I said, I have to work. What do you want me to do, Vee?"

What I wanted her to do was go with me. She had missed everything in San Francisco because she'd had to work. I guess that was a good thing, since we'd lost, but I still wanted her with me tomorrow. I wanted her to do things with me sometimes and not always worry about working and money and bills.

But I didn't say that. I just put my head down.

"Look . . ." I could tell Mama felt a little bad when she started talking in that softer voice. "I'm sorry I can't go, but

19

that doesn't have anything to do with you. You go on and have a good time. Big Mama will watch the boys."

"But it won't be the same if you're not there. Diamond's gonna be there with her mother. And India—"

My mother held up her hand. "I don't want to hear it." Now she had that mad voice. "I'm working tomorrow, and that's that. Now get on out of here."

"Yeah, leave your mother alone!"

"You leave her alone, D'Wayne," Mama said to him.

"I'm just sayin', she needs to let you relax."

I rolled my eyes—making sure my mother didn't see me—and stomped right past the both of them.

"You better pick up your feet," my mother said. Her mad voice was even louder now.

I knew she wasn't playing, so I did exactly what she said. But that didn't stop *me* from being mad. I wanted to slam my door so bad, but I wasn't crazy. I put my headphones back on and banged on my keyboard.

I didn't really know why I was so mad. I mean, my mother did work hard—I didn't know anybody who worked like she did. Sometimes, after a full shift at the hospital as a nurse's aide, she would go to her part-time gig with Execu-Fresh and clean the offices in all of those big corporate buildings near the airport. She hardly ever took any days off.

I didn't even know I was crying until my tears dripped down on my keyboard. I got up and turned off the light.

Lying down on my bed, I could hear my brothers in their room next to mine, laughing and rolling around. I guess they were watching their new TV. I just knew in a minute, my mom would go in there and start yelling for them to be quiet. But my brothers kept making all that noise, and my mama didn't do a thing. I guess she was still in the living room . . . hugged up with D'Wayne.

I had to find my father.

I rolled over in my bed, trying to think of some way to do that. My mother wouldn't help me—I knew that. She'd probably even tell me not to do it. Maybe Pastor Ford could help. It was always so easy to talk to her—and she never said no to anything—at least not directly. She always asked what you thought was best and if she asked me that, I would tell her that it would be best if I found my father.

That's what I would do. I would tell Pastor my plans to go to New York. And she would never let me go by myself; she'd go with me.

I closed my eyes and said a prayer asking God to help me come up with the right words to say to Pastor Ford tomorrow.

Then I said a special prayer asking God to bless my father.

Chapter Four

"So, for real, you're not going to ride with me?"

Even though our heads were bowed as Pastor Ford gave the benediction, my best sistah, Diamond, was still gabbin' as if the church service was already over.

I waited until Pastor said, "Amen," before I lifted my head, looked at my sistah, and told her for the hundredth time that I wasn't going to ride with her.

Diamond leaned against the balcony railing. "Why not?" she whined just like my brothers did when they didn't get their way.

But I wasn't hardly backing down. I had a plan, and Diamond wasn't part of it. "Because I told you, I have something to do before the dinner."

She crossed her arms and looked me up and down. "Whatever, whatever. Don't say I didn't give you the big chance." She lowered her voice. "I wanted you to be first to ride in my car, but. . . ." She turned and grinned all in India and Aaliyah's faces. "So, y'all want me to pick you up for dinner tonight?"

When India and Aaliyah shook their heads, I thought Diamond was going to have one of her heart attacks.

"Why're y'all doing this to me? You're supposed to be my crew. Ride or die. When I roll, you roll. Remember?"

"I am riding . . . with my mom," India said.

I didn't want to laugh, but I had to. India sure had changed since she'd lost all that weight.

Diamond sucked her teeth and turned to Aaliyah.

Aaliyah shrugged. "I'm rolling with my dad."

"What's up with all this hanging out with the parents stuff?" Diamond asked. "That's so not cool."

"It was cool enough for you until this morning," Aaliyah said.

Diamond's smile was back. "Actually, it was cool until last night at seven-eighteen. That was the exact moment when my dad gave me these." Diamond held up a set of car keys.

We'd been in church for two hours, and Diamond had shown us those keys at least one hundred times. But even though she was starting to get on my nerves with dangling those keys in my face, I was excited, and I knew India and Aaliyah were happy, too.

We'd been grinning as hard as she had been this morning when she'd busted into the choir room where we hung out before church and jingled those keys in the air. "Here they are!" she had screamed. "The keys to my new car!"

We'd all heard about Diamond's new car. She'd called India and Aaliyah last night. And then she'd called me this morning when she'd been sure that I (and not the Queen) would answer the phone.

So we all knew the story of how her mother and father had given her a new car right after dinner. But I wasn't hardly surprised. I'd been way more surprised when she hadn't gotten a car on Christmas Eve for her birthday.

24

Diamond had been shocked, too—especially when her parents had told her that it was going to be a little while before she got one.

"We have to make sure you're ready. That you're going to be responsible." That's what Diamond told us her mother had said.

I guess losing made you responsible. 'Cause I was sure that was why Diamond's parents had bought her that car. Last week, when we'd lost in San Francisco, Diamond had cried so hard, I thought she was gonna have a heart attack—and not one of those pretend ones that she faked all the time.

And the way she was pouting and holding her hand over her chest, I began to wonder if she was going to have a real heart attack now.

So I said, "I could use a ride home tonight after the dinner. My mom's gotta work, and I was gonna ask Pastor—"

Diamond's grin was so big her cheeks had to be hurting. "Don't do that! I got you, girl."

We were the last ones to clear out of the balcony, and as we headed down the back stairs, India asked, "Why didn't you drive this morning? I sure wanted to see your car."

"I wanted to ride one more time with my parents. But after today, it's on!" She swung her hair over her shoulder.

We were at the bottom of the stairs when Aaliyah said, "Knowing your mom and dad, they probably didn't *let* you drive."

Diamond turned around and moved her head in a sistah-girl kind of way. "My parents don't *let* me do anything. I'm sixteen. I'm grown and I'm known. And now that I have a car, I'll come and go as I please."

"Is that so?"

Not one of us had heard Mr. Linden step up. I stood still, kinda scared of what he might say. I mean, he was a nice man and everything, but all I could think about was what my mom would do if she'd heard me talking like that.

With a frown, Mr. Linden said, "So, you're gonna come and go as you please, huh?" But hardly a second passed before he started cracking up.

I let out a long breath and laughed right along with them. When Diamond hugged her dad, I kinda got a tingly feeling. That's exactly the way I knew my father would hug me.

"You might have a car, young lady," Mr. Linden said, "but you're still my little girl. And you won't be coming and going as you please. Not as long—"

"I know, Daddy," Diamond interrupted him. "Not as long as I live in your house." She rolled her eyes, but there was still a big ole grin on her face. Like she was really happy—about her car and about her dad.

"You got that right. Now are you ready to go?"

"Uh-huh." She waved at us. "Holla!" And then when her father turned away, she added in a low voice, "The next time you see me, I'll be rollin' in *my* car!" before she ran to catch up with Mr. Linden.

I watched Diamond take her dad's hand, and I wished for the day when I'd be walking next to my father and he would have his arms around me—just like that.

I prayed to God that day would come soon.

Chapter Five

It was a long walk up this hill, but it was worth it.

I didn't even mind that I had taken two buses to get here. Not a bit of that mattered, as long as I was going to have some time with Pastor Ford. Even though I was in good shape, I was huffing and puffing by the time I got to Pastor's door.

I looked at my watch. Perfect. No one else would be here for another hour. I got my lie together, took off my headphones, and rang the doorbell.

"Hey, Veronique," Pastor said with surprise all in her voice. She frowned, just a little.

"Hi." And then, as part of my act, I frowned right back. "What's wrong?"

"Nothing. You're just a little early. But come on in."

I opened my eyes all big. "Early? I thought you said three."

Pastor's forehead was really filled with lines now. The way she stared, like she was looking right through me, made me like crazy-nervous.

Then when she said, "Veronique Garrett," I knew the gig

was up. "You don't have to lie to come to my home. You're always welcome here. Don't you know that?"

"Yes, Pastor. But I thought—"

Pastor held up her hand. "You didn't *think* anything, so don't even *think* about standing here telling another bold-faced lie right to my face."

Did I feel busted! I should've known that Pastor would figure it out. She always knew what was up.

She grabbed my hand. "I'm glad you're early. I need some company."

Okay, that was one of the things I loved about her. She could bust you all up against the wall, but in the next second, she was like your BFF.

"Where's Gail?" I wondered if Pastor Ford's daughter was home. Not that Gail being here would stop me, 'cause Gail was crazy-cool and not really that much older than I was. She would definitely understand me wanting to find my dad.

"She's out, so you can help me get ready." Pastor Ford led me straight into the kitchen. I didn't say a word while Pastor showed me how she wanted the plates stacked on the table and the napkins folded. I did it all while she stirred whatever was smelling so good in that big black pot. Then she checked on some other stuff in the oven.

For a long time, we didn't say a word, but I still felt good. I always did around my pastor. Not only did I like being in her house 'cause it was all that, but she rocked, too. Sometimes when I started wondering if I would ever find my father, I thought about what it would be like to live with Pastor Ford. Diamond always said that she treated me like I was her kid.

"Pastor Ford likes you better than the rest of us. Like you're her daughter or something."

"No, she doesn't!" That's what I always said whenever

Diamond brought that up. But truth—I was feelin' that. Not that I didn't love my mother. Trust and know. But Pastor was so different—she had her life together, and because of that, she always had time for me.

"So, how's everything? How's school?"

See, that's exactly what I was talking about. My mother never asked me anything like that.

"School's fine. I'm thinking about getting back in the student government since . . ." It was hard to say it out loud, really hard to admit that the Divine Divas had lost. I took a deep breath and finished, "Since I don't have to worry about practicing anymore."

"I think it's good for you girls to be involved in school. But you gave up being the sophomore class president, right?"

I nodded. "Yeah, but I was thinking about getting involved with the political action team. It should be pretty interesting with the elections."

Pastor Ford put the spoon down and smiled. "That's a good idea. I was thinking about having you help me organize something at the church. A get-out-and-vote campaign or something."

"That would be great, Pastor," I said, thinking how much fun it would be to work on something with her. We'd have to spend all kinds of time together planning. "I've got an idea," I said. "Maybe we can do something like have a panel. And we can get people from the church to study what all of the candidates think. And then, we could have a program. And someone would represent each candidate. And then, they would give their opinion so that everyone will know what each candidate thinks. Maybe we could call it a caucus—like in Iowa. We'll have our own. Or maybe we can just call it a debate and. . . ."

"Hold up." Pastor Ford laughed and waved her hands in the air. "That sounds great, though I have to check out our nonprofit status and see what we can do. But we don't have to plan it all today, do we?"

Okay, so maybe I was going a little over the top. But who wouldn't? I mean, Pastor Ford had just asked me to help her organize something major, something that could take the place of the Divine Divas. Now I would have something to look forward to, something more than just going home and taking care of my brothers.

"I'll tell you what," Pastor Ford said. "Let's meet this week."

"Okay."

"So, what else is on your mind?"

See! With Pastor, it was all about me. I didn't have to say anything for her to know everything.

"Well, there is something." I stopped and thought about exactly how I wanted to tell her about my dad. "It's . . ." Before I could get another word out, the bell rang.

Dang it!

Pastor rushed to the door, leaving me standing in the kitchen. I looked at the clock—I couldn't believe I had wasted thirty minutes, but I still should've had another thirty minutes. Who was stepping in on my time?

"Vee!"

Diamond! Why was she here so early? By the time I got to the front, I saw what was up. The door was wide open, and Pastor and Diamond were outside. Both of them were admiring her new car.

Of course, I wanted to see the car, but couldn't Diamond have come at four o'clock, like she was supposed to?

As I stood at the door, Diamond waved to me. "Pastor told me you were here already. Come and see my car!"

30

I wasn't happy about this—until I got closer. My mouth was wide open as I stared at the bright red car.

This morning, when Diamond had told me her parents had given her a Honda, I'd been a little surprised. I mean, I thought my girl would only roll in a BMW or something. But now I knew why she was so excited. This wasn't any ordinary Honda. This was one of those tricked-out sport coupes with tinted windows, sparkles in the paint, and shiny, eighteen-inch Sterns, shaped like diamonds.

"So what do you think?" Diamond asked me.

"I . . . it's . . ." I had no words.

"We're gonna be lookin' fly and rollin' phat!"

I was still standing there when India and Ms. Tova drove up and started "oohing" and "aahhing" around the car, just like Pastor. A few minutes later, Aaliyah and Mr. Heber arrived. Right after that, Diamond's parents came, and they stood around the car, too, like this was the first time they were seeing it.

We were hanging out on the sidewalk, laughing and talking for so long that Pastor Ford finally said, "Let's take this party inside."

We packed into the house and when Pastor asked us to take a seat, all the laughing stopped. By the time the grown-ups sat and my sistahs and I were on the floor, it got real quiet. Like everybody remembered why we were there. I felt bad all over again.

Pastor Ford began, "I was going to play this out, but by the looks on your faces, I need to just tell you the news."

I glanced at my sistahs. Their faces were all scrunched up like mine. Even my girl Aaliyah, who didn't want to be a Divine Diva in the first place, was looking all sad.

"I said this was a celebration. And it is. You ladies have got to know how proud we are of you."

I think it was Aaliyah's dad who started clapping first. Then all the grown-ups joined in. It was kind of weird to have people clapping even though we were sitting in Pastor's house and not on some stage. I guess they were just trying to make us feel better. But the applause only reminded me that this was the last time anybody would be clapping for us.

I put a big ole grin on my face anyway. When I looked around, Diamond, India, and Aaliyah were wearing stupid smiles, too.

Pastor Ford waited for the clapping to stop. "This is a party to celebrate everything you girls accomplished. And"—she spread her arms open wide—"this is a party to celebrate the Divine Divas being back in the competition!"

The grown-ups started clapping again. They were wearing big grins like they understood what Pastor Ford was saying. But to me, she sounded like she was speaking another language, because I surely understood English and I didn't understand a word she was saying right now. From the looks on their faces, my sistahs were confused, too.

Pastor said it again. "The Divine Divas are back in the competition."

Diamond was the first to stand up, like she got it. And then India and Aaliyah did. I only stood up because my sistahs had.

"What do you mean, Pastor?"

I was so glad Aaliyah asked that question, because right about now, I had one of those inquiring minds, and I wanted to know.

"The Faithful Five, who won the competition in San Francisco, has been eliminated. One of their members is twenty-one. That's three years over the age limit."

"So . . . so . . . so . . ." Diamond stuttered like she didn't know any other words. And it wasn't like India, Aaliyah, or I could help her out.

"So, it turns out that the Divine Divas came in second—or, actually, first. That means you." Pastor Ford pointed to Diamond and then turned to us, "and you and you and you—are going to New York to compete in the semifinals." She was clapping before she even finished the sentence.

That was the first time the words made sense. By the time I opened my mouth to cheer, my sistahs were already screaming. We hugged and we danced. And then we hugged some more.

How great was this? We were back to being the Divine Divas, and we were going to New York.

It was on now!

For the next two hours, we celebrated—exactly the way Pastor Ford wanted us to.

I sat on the floor with my girls in a circle, while the grown-ups hung out in the kitchen. They were making more noise than we were with their talking and laughing.

"Can you believe it?" India kept saying and shaking her head.

"I can believe it. Remember, we prayed." I reminded my sistahs how we'd had prayed really hard right after we'd lost in San Francisco.

Aaliyah said, "Yeah, we prayed and kissed it up to God."

That part had been Aaliyah's idea—to say the prayer and then kiss it up to God like we used to do when we were little kids and dropped candy on the floor. But truth—I'd thought that was stupid when Aaliyah had told us to do it; I'd only done it because she was my sistah. It didn't look so stupid now.

"Do you think God took this away from that other group?" India asked.

"He didn't have to," Aaliyah said. "They cheated. They took it away from themselves."

"Pastor said something good was going to come out of this." Diamond laughed. "I told you that we were born to be stars. Maybe now y'all will listen to me."

"I'm going to call my dad! He's in Chicago." India reached for her cell phone, and as she did, the one little chicken wing she had on her plate slipped. She tried to catch it, but it dropped to the floor. "Shoot!"

"That's okay," Aaliyah said, picking up the meat. "We'll just kiss it up to God."

Diamond and I laughed as Aaliyah brushed the chicken against her lips, raised it in the air, then handed it to India.

"Ewww. I'm not gonna eat that now."

"Why not?" I asked. "We're sistahs, right?"

"Well . . . , maybe." But she still pushed her plate to the side before she flipped open her cell.

While Diamond and Aaliyah kept talking about New York, I listened to India talk to her father. Not in a staring-in-her-mouth listening kind of way. I just slowly chewed some macaroni and cheese and pretended that I wasn't listening. But I heard every word India said. And I heard her father cheer right through the phone.

I couldn't wait until I'd be calling my father with good stuff like this.

When India hung up from her father, Diamond whispered to me, "This is boring. You ready to get out of here?"

Diamond wasn't hardly bored. Truth—she couldn't wait to get me into her car.

On the real, though, I was ready to leave, too. My mom

was still at work, but I wanted to be home the moment she got there so that I could tell her this great news.

Diamond and I grabbed our sweaters, but before we could start saying 'bye, Pastor pulled me and my sistahs together in the living room.

"There's one last thing I want to talk about." The big-time grin Pastor had had on all day was gone. The way she looked, I began to wonder if she was going to say something like *"April Fool's"* and tell us that we weren't really going to New York.

My chest was hurting bad with the way my heart was pounding.

"You girls will have a lot on your plate with school and practice . . ."

"We can handle it," Diamond piped in like she was the diva-in-charge, or something.

"I have a lot of confidence that you can," Pastor said. "But sometimes, life gets heavy, and I want you to know that if there is ever anything going on, if anything ever gets too much for you, you always have a place to come. To your parents. To Sybil. To me. We are always here to help you. No judgment— all you'll ever get from us is love."

What was she talking about? And then I figured it out. I looked over at India—this was about her and what had happened right before the San Francisco trip. Her stomach had ruptured because she'd been throwing up.

I didn't want to stare at India like I was blaming this whole lecture on her. So I just kept peeking at her through the corner of my eye. She was staring straight at Pastor like she didn't have a thing to hide.

Good for her! India used to be the quiet one, but ever since she lost all that weight, she's had lots of confidence— not loads, like Diamond, but enough, almost as much as me and Aaliyah. Looked like that head doctor her mother was still dragging her to was working, although it still didn't look like she was eating all that much.

"Okay, well, you have school tomorrow, and we've had quite a night. . . ."

"Yes," Diamond jumped up before Pastor Ford even finished, "I'm ready to go." When Pastor raised her eyebrows, Diamond added, "I didn't mean that. I just—"

Pastor held up her hand. "I know what you meant." She laughed before she gave Diamond a hug. "You can't wait to get in your car. Well, go on. Just be safe."

"Veronique." Pastor pulled me to the side while Diamond went into the kitchen to say 'bye to her parents. "Wasn't there something else you wanted to talk about?"

I had forgotten all about that—the reason why I'd come to Pastor's house so early. But there was no need to have that talk about my dad. Now that we were going to New York, I had the whole thing under control.

"No, Pastor," I lied. "There was nothing else."

"Well, I want you to know that even though the Divine Divas are back in the competition, you can stay focused on school and those other activities we talked about."

I couldn't give up my job now. I needed all the money I could get my hands on, 'cause there was no way my mom was going to pay for that trip.

"You don't have to worry about the money," Pastor said, reading my mind like she always did. "I met with the executive board, and Hope Chapel is going to take care of everything for you girls."

I wanted to cry as I hugged my pastor. "Thank you," I whispered in her ear.

"You're more than welcome." She pulled back from me. "I

believe in you girls. I want to give you the best chance to go all the way."

As Diamond and I walked to the door, her mother followed right behind us.

"Be careful," Ms. Elizabeth warned.

"Yes, Mother. But I drove over here. I'm fine."

Diamond's mother didn't even hear her. "And no talking on the phone while you're driving."

"Yes, Mother. But—"

"And no speeding. Watch all the traffic signs."

Diamond gave up. This time, she only said, "Yes, Mother."

Then Ms. Elizabeth turned to me. "And both of you, wear your seat belts."

We said, "Yes," together, but I let Diamond add the "Mother" part.

Then she was right back at Diamond. "And after you drop Vee off, come straight home. Remember, you can't be out driving alone after midnight."

"It's only seven, Mother. And anyway, you and Daddy never let me stay out past ten."

"Okay, then, drive responsibly."

Dang! If having a car came with this many rules, I wasn't sure I wanted one.

I didn't think we were ever going to get into that car, but when we finally did, I had never felt seats so soft.

"What kind of leather is this?"

"The expensive kind." Diamond laughed.

The seats were all that, but the dashboard was even better. All of those silver knobs and handles made the car look like some kind of super spaceship. I shook my head. It was amazing what rich people could do.

We were only two minutes out of her mother's sight when

Diamond plugged in her MP3 player and put Soulja Boy on blast.

"What were you and Pastor talking about?" Diamond screamed over the music.

Okay, riding with my sistah was crazy-cool, but I didn't think losing my hearing needed to be part of the deal—especially not listening to this guy. "I don't like this song," I said, turning down the music.

Diamond frowned. "Why not?"

" 'Cause if you listen to the words, you'd know that song is derogatory to women."

Diamond leaned back and looked at me. "Derogatory to women? You sound like Aaliyah."

I stared at her, letting my sistah know that I wasn't playing.

"Whatever, whatever!" She switched to Fergie and turned the music back up. "You take this stuff too seriously," she yelled.

"And you should, too." I turned the music down again. "Do you want to hear what Pastor told me or not?"

"Go 'head," she said like she didn't care.

But I didn't care if she wanted to hear it or not. I couldn't wait to tell her. "Pastor said not to worry about working. The church is going to pay our way to New York."

"That's awesome, Vee," she said, turning the volume back up. "You shouldn't be working anyway," she yelled. "We're too young to be doing anything except having fun." And then she started singing so loud that I couldn't hear Fergie anymore. " 'The glamorous, glamorous life!' "

I sighed. That's all it was about for my sistah—fun and glamour. But that was her life, not mine. At least not yet.

"Speaking of fun, have you seen that new guy in school?" she asked.

Like there was only one new guy. "Who are you talking about?"

"Arjay!" Like I should have known. "He is *so* fine."

Was there a boy on earth that Diamond didn't think was fine?

When I didn't say anything, she said, "You know Arjay Lennox. The new guy in our homeroom. I don't know much about him, but I heard he just transferred here from Chicago. His father's job relocated them, and they're living somewhere in Beverly Hills, so you know they got money. And he has an older brother, but I haven't seen him. I wonder if he's as fine as Arjay."

"I thought you didn't know much about him."

Diamond laughed. "I don't, but give me a minute." She winked at me and went right back to her singing.

I had to laugh at my sistah. When she put her mind on something, she always got it. And it looked like she had her mind all over this new boy.

I knew who she was talking about, and, like Diamond said, Arjay was cute. But I didn't have time to think about any boys. Not that I didn't think some of them were cool; but right now, there were way too many other things on my mind.

I just hoped that this boy didn't get in the way of the Divine Divas like Diamond's first obsession—Jax Xavier. Because of their relationship, Diamond's parents almost pulled her out of the competition. I needed to keep my girl straight so that nothing messed up New York.

"I hope we get to go to New York a couple of days early," I said.

Now Diamond turned down the music. "We have to. It's like a five-hour flight, so we need at least a day to rest up."

"Cool."

"Girl, the NYC is so fab; it's so much more sophisticated

than L.A. And the shopping on Fifth Avenue is all that. Trust."

"I just hope we all stay focused this time. I don't want any more drama messing us up."

"You mean like India getting sick last time?"

"I mean like you," I said, looking right at her, "getting grounded because of Jax."

She waved her hand at me. "I am so over Jax it's not even funny."

But before I could tell her he wasn't the one I was worried about, we turned onto my block. Right away, I stopped thinking about everything when I peeped the sight in front of me.

My mom was almost skipping as she ran down the steps, holding D'Wayne's hand.

"I thought your mom was working."

I was hoping that Diamond hadn't seen her. "She was. Maybe she got off early," I said, even though I didn't believe that. My mom never left work early. Not even when one of us got sick. If something ever happened, Big Mama was the one who took care of us.

Diamond pulled the Honda over to the curb and leaned forward like she was trying to get a better look through the window. "Who's that with her?"

I closed my eyes, praying that my mom and D'Wayne would walk faster so Diamond wouldn't figure it out.

"Oh, my God! Don't tell me that the Queen is hanging out with El Creepo again," she said, calling D'Wayne by the name she'd given him a couple of years ago.

I was so busted! I didn't want Diamond to know D'Wayne was back, because she knew the whole history. Since he started coming around when I was little, I told Diamond every time he left and every time he came back—except for this time. I don't know why, but this time, I was really embarrassed for my mom. Like this time, by letting D'Wayne back, she looked really stupid.

"It is him!" Diamond said, hitting her hand on the steering wheel. When my mom and D'Wayne walked around the corner and out of sight, my sistah screamed at me, "Why didn't you tell me?"

I shrugged. "Wasn't nothing to tell."

"Well, I hope you told your mother!"

I shrugged again. "Wasn't nothing to tell her, either."

"What? You have a lot to tell her."

"What am I supposed to say? That I think he's a loser? She already knows that."

"No, she doesn't. Not if she's still hanging out with him." She took a breath. "You need to tell her what you told me— that he creeps you out."

That's what I'd told Diamond the last time D'Wayne had come back. I couldn't remember ever liking him, but suddenly, he was like crazy-creepy to me. It had started that day when I'd been taking a shower and he'd come into the bathroom.

"Oh, I'm sorry, Lil' Mama," he had said to me when I'd stepped out of the tub and screamed. "I just had to use the toilet, bad."

What's wrong with the bathroom in Mama's room? was what I'd thought to myself. But I hadn't said nothin' 'cause I'd just wanted him out of there.

Then the next day right before I was leaving for school, he'd said, "So, you're wearing a bra now, huh, Lil' Mama? How old're you? Twelve, thirteen?"

I hadn't even answered him. Just walked right out that door and told Diamond the moment I got to school. She'd told me then to tell my mom, but I hadn't been sure. Mama was always so happy when D'Wayne was around, and I hadn't wanted to be the one to make her sad. And anyway, a few weeks later, just like always, he'd been gone.

"You need to tell the Queen, Vee!" Diamond screamed through my memories.

I had a feeling my sistah was right, but what was I supposed to say? That I didn't like the way he looked at me? Or that I didn't like the way he sometimes got too close? Or that sometimes I caught him staring at me when I wasn't looking? The only thing my mother would have said was, "So what?"

I shook my head. "She'll just say that I'm being stupid and he'll still be here anyway. And that will make it worse."

Diamond looked at me for a long time before she said, "I hear you."

The way she said it made me feel bad. Like she felt sorry for me or something. I was sorry that I'd ever told Diamond all those stories about D'Wayne, 'cause now I was embarrassed. Of my mother. Of D'Wayne. Of not having my father around. Of everything.

"I'll catch you tomorrow." I opened the car door fast; I couldn't wait to get out of there.

"Wanna ride to school?"

"I thought your parents weren't letting you drive to school."

"I'm not supposed to, but if you need a ride, I might be able to talk my dad and the judge into it."

I shook my head. "Don't be using me."

"A girl's gotta try." She laughed, turned up the music again, waved, and drove away.

I stood on the street until I couldn't hear Fergie's beat anymore.

I couldn't remember a time when I felt so bad. Not only was my mom hanging with that loser, but she had also lied to me. She'd said she had to work. But that hadn't been true. All she'd wanted to do was hang with D'Wayne.

It was like she had no love for me, even though I really tried—working hard in school, staying home with my brothers. I did everything she asked me to do. But it wasn't enough.

This was just another reason that I had to get to New York. Because I knew for sure that when I found my father, *he* would love me.

Chapter Six

I clicked off the television the moment I heard the key in the lock. The door was barely open before D'Andre, who was always the ringleader, barged in. And my other brothers followed him, screaming loud.

"Y'all stop that noise!"

My mother came into the apartment, carrying two shopping bags. Right behind her was D'Wayne, with his arms filled with bags, too.

"Hey, Mama." I didn't say a word to or even look at D'Wayne.

"Hey, baby." She sounded like she was tired when she let the bags fall on the counter.

I waited to see if she was going to ask me about Pastor's party.

"Come and help me put away these groceries," was all she said.

I looked at D'Wayne and wondered why he couldn't help. But he was already spread out on the couch. He picked up the remote, clicked on the TV, flipped through a few channels, then blasted *Beavis and Butt-Head* through the apartment.

I started filling the shelves with the cans from one of the bags.

When my mother still didn't ask me anything, I said, "Mama, Pastor gave us some great news today."

"Really, baby?"

"Yeah. We're going to New York."

For the first time since she'd come home, my mother smiled. "New York? The Divine Divas?"

"Uh-huh." I explained to her how we were back in the contest. "We start practice again on Tuesday."

"That's great." Her smile didn't stay very long. "Now, Vee, you know I don't have any New York money." When she took a breath, I already knew what she was going to say next. "I'm not about to spend money I don't have."

"That's okay, Mama. Pastor said . . ." Something made me stop. "You don't need to have the money, Mama, I'm still going to be working at the church," I lied.

I felt kinda bad about lying to my mother. It's not something that I did a lot. But she had just lied to me about having to work today, so now we were even.

"Is that little job going to be enough money for New York?"

"Yeah, I'm gonna put in more hours, and Pastor said it would be enough." I wasn't too worried about my mom finding out the truth. Whenever D'Wayne came back, she never went to church, so she wouldn't see Pastor for a few months.

"I don't want you taking any handouts, Vee. We don't need nothin' from nobody."

How could she say that? She'd just given me the we-have-no-money lecture, so we needed something from somebody.

"I'm not taking anything. Working at the bookstore, especially extra days, will give me enough money for New York."

"Well, if you have New York money, then you need to give me and your mama a little something to help out around here."

Slowly, I turned to that voice. D'Wayne wasn't even looking at me, but his mouth was moving like he was supposed to be in my business. *Give you a little something? Dude, what're you talking about?*

Before I could put him right in his place, Mama said, "Whatever money Vee earns is for her and the Divine Divas. I told her that before."

"Well, it's okay if she keeps that little money," D'Wayne said as if he had anything to do with me. "But if she wins that contest, things are gonna change around here."

If my mother wasn't standing right there and if I thought God wouldn't hear me, I would've cursed him out.

D'Wayne just kept on talking. "I need to know what's going on with that contest. Have you signed any papers yet?"

What I wanted to do was ignore him, but Mama didn't play that. So I just asked him, "Why do you want to know?" with enough attitude to make him stop his roll right there.

But that didn't stop a thing. He said, "I need to make sure everything is on the up-and-up with the money."

"It's not your money!"

"It is as long as you live in this house."

My mouth opened wide. *This house?* As if he lived here. As if he planned to stay. As if.

I turned to my mother knowing for sure that she was going to tell D'Wayne to mind his business. But all she did was close the refrigerator and say, "Vee, after you finish putting these away, check on your brothers for me, please. Make sure they're ready for bed." Then she flopped down right next to

D'Wayne. She didn't even change the channels—just watched *Beavis and Butt-Head* with him.

After I finished with the groceries, I walked past my mother and D'Wayne, slowing down so that I could tell D'Wayne what I really thought about him—with my eyes, not my mouth. They didn't even look up as I headed to my brothers' bedroom.

D'Marcus looked like he was already sleeping, but D'Andre and D'Angelo were on their bunk beds, watching TV. I couldn't believe that they were watching the same thing that D'Wayne and Mama were watching.

I peeked into the crib that Mama had rolled from her bedroom into theirs ever since D'Wayne had come back. My little brother was knocked out.

Then I said to the twins, "Mama said for you guys to go to sleep."

"Ah, shut up!" D'Andre jumped down from his bunk and pushed me out of the room.

No problem. I didn't want to deal with them anyway.

Inside my bedroom, I put on my headphones, hooked up my MP3, and cued up to my favorite song. I listened to Natasha sing and thought about everything—New York, D'Wayne, but most of all, I thought about my dad. I listened to the song for so long that I finally had an idea and a plan.

I knew exactly how I was going to find my father.

Chapter Seven

I was dreaming about my father again.

Then I heard the knock on the door, but I didn't want to wake up. I wanted to stay right there in my bed.

But when my mom called out, "Vee!" I knew I had to get up. It was like this every morning; I had to get up early to get my brothers ready for school while Mama dressed for work.

I yawned. "I'm coming."

Mama opened my door. "I just wanted to make sure you were up."

I frowned. Why was my mother already dressed in her white uniform? "You want me to make breakfast for D'Andre and 'em?"

She sat on the edge of my bed. "Nope. Your brothers are already gone."

When I looked at the clock, my mouth opened wide. It was after seven. I never slept this late on a school day. Mama always made sure that I was up by six. Then, after I got my brothers ready, she would take D'Andre, D'Angelo, and

D'Marcus to school before she dropped D'Wight off at Big Mama's house.

If it was this late, something bad must've happened. But my mother was smiling.

"Where are they?" I asked about my brothers.

"D'Wayne took them."

I guess it was automatic, because when I heard his name, I rolled my eyes.

Mama took a deep breath. "I know you don't like D'Wayne, but you need to make an effort to get along with him."

I wanted to tell my mother that the only way I was ever going to get along with D'Wayne was if he lived in an igloo in Alaska and stayed there until the end of time.

My mother said, "I told him the same thing about you. Both of you need to work on getting along."

That was never going to happen.

"Remember, he's your brothers' father."

I felt sorry for them.

"That means something to me." She stopped for a second. "Vee, I grew up without my father and I hate that the same thing has happened to you. I know you miss him."

That was a big wow for me! I never knew Mama thought anything about me missing my dad at all.

She said, "I know D'Wayne comes and goes, but every time he's here, your brothers get a little piece of their father. To me, that's better than what you and I got. That's better than nothing at all."

Now that made me think a little. I mean, he was my brothers' father. And maybe when he was gone, they missed him, just like I missed my dad.

"And he makes me happy, Vee."

Just when I was beginning to feel this whole missing father thing, Mama had to go ruin it by saying that. How could he make her happy when every time he left, he made her sad?

"He doesn't make you happy," I protested. "In a couple of months, he'll be gone and you'll be upset again."

"That's not gonna happen this time."

This was one of those days when I felt like the mother, and Mama was the kid. Whenever my mother talked to me about D'Wayne, she sounded way younger than me.

"D'Wayne is my soul mate," my mother said.

Oh, brother.

She said, "Why do you think he keeps coming back?"

"Why does he keep leaving?"

Mama shook her head as if she didn't like what I'd just said. But I didn't care. I said, "He never treats you right."

My mother made a long sigh sound. Even though it was morning, she sounded so tired. "You don't know what it's like—two jobs, five kids." She stopped for a moment. "Now, you know I love you all, but when D'Wayne's here, it's nice, it's easier."

I knew it was hard for her; that's why I always did everything I could to help out. "Mama, it's not like you're alone. I can help you."

"You already help a lot."

"But I can do more. I can get a job and then maybe you won't have to clean those buildings. You can just work at the hospital. And I can help out even more with D'Andre and 'em."

She brushed her hand on my cheek. "You're so sweet, Vee. Sometimes I forget that. But how are you going to get another job? You already have a job at the church, and I'm not going to have *you* working two jobs, too."

I'd almost forgotten about my lie. Now I wished I hadn't told her that. But I couldn't go back on that; if my mother knew I'd lied, she'd be crazy-mad.

"And anyway, you already have enough," Mama continued. "With school, your job, the Divine Divas, I don't want you worrying about anything else. I want you to just be a teenager."

"But I wanna help, Mama. I want you to tell D'Wayne . . ." I stopped.

She said, "Tell D'Wayne what? Tell him to leave?"

As bad as I wanted to say yes, I didn't.

Mama said, "Don't you want me to be happy?"

Of course that's what I wanted. I nodded but didn't say another word. There was no use saying anything else; she wasn't hearing me.

Anyway, I didn't know why I was trippin' so hard. When I found my dad and he came back, he would be her soul mate. And he would meet my brothers and he would be their father. And not one of us would ever have a single, solitary thought about D'Wayne ever again.

"Okay, it's time to get up," Mama said. "Big Mama will be bringing the boys home at six. Is that going to work with your schedule?"

"Uh-huh," I said, not feeling so bad anymore about lying because now I was lying for her, too. Her life was going to be so much better because of me.

"Okay, I'll see you tonight."

When my mother closed my door, I leaned back in my bed and thought about my plan. All I had to do now was hook up with Diamond.

I hadn't said anything to her yesterday, but now I was ready. Diamond was my best sistah, and she would help me. And a little help was all that I needed.

Chapter Eight

"Hurry up!"

Diamond was struggling with the key in the lock.

"What's taking you so long?" I asked.

She rolled her eyes. "Maybe it's because you're rushing me."

"Finally," I said when she opened the door. I dashed straight up the staircase to Diamond's bedroom.

"What is wrong with you?" Diamond huffed up the steps far behind me.

I flopped down on her bed and waited. What was taking her so long? I mean, yeah, I had made her run all the way home from school. And yeah, it was like twelve blocks or something like that. But dang, she used to be a cheerleader; she should've been able to keep up with a sistah.

When Diamond finally came into the room, she dumped her Gucci messenger bag on the bed and put her hands on her hips. "So, you gonna tell me what's going down?" she asked, still out of breath.

"I need a solid."

"What?"

"I need to use your computer."

Diamond frowned. "You made me run all the way home so that you can do some homework?" The way she sucked her teeth and crossed her arms, I knew she was crazy-mad.

"I didn't say a single solitary thing about homework." I took a deep breath. "I have something to tell you, but you have to *promise* not to tell *anyone*."

My best sistah wasn't looking so mad anymore. She bounced down on the bed. "I won't tell a soul," she whispered, even though there was no one else in the house.

"Okay, this is a *big* secret."

"Yeah?" Her eyes were wide; she couldn't wait. "Tell me!"

I opened my mouth, but all of a sudden, I wasn't so sure that I wanted to tell Diamond. I mean, she was my best friend and all that, but could I really trust a sistah not to say anything?

Then I got an idea. "Okay, I'll tell you, but first, you've got to tell *me* a secret."

She frowned. "Hold up. This is about you. How did I get all in it?"

"Just tell me something—something you've never told anyone else."

"Why?"

"Because then I'll know something about you and I'll be sure that you won't tell my secret."

"But I wouldn't tell anyone anyway. I can keep a secret." She stopped. "Trust and know."

I guess Diamond thought using my words would convince me. But I wasn't going out like that. I was sticking to it—a secret for a secret.

I folded my arms and stared her down.

She glared right back at me.

I shrugged. "If you don't want to know."

"Okay, okay!" She gave in. "I'll tell."

Of course she would. Me—the boring one of the crew—having a secret was just too juicy for Diamond to let it go.

"I got something," she said. The way she bit her lip and blinked her eyes had me a little curious. She was acting like she was about to tell me something major.

She said, "You can't tell anybody."

"I won't." Now I was the one who couldn't wait.

"I"—she lowered her eyes and her voice—"slept with Jax."

It took me a minute. "Slept with? Like sex?"

She nodded.

"What!"

"Ssshhh!" Diamond put her hand over my mouth.

I could hardly breathe, but that didn't stop me from talking. "I thought you stopped seeing him. When did you sleep with him?"

"A long time ago."

Dang, and I'd been worried about my sistah keeping a secret. Please! She'd kept a big ole one.

She said, "Remember back in November when I got grounded?"

I nodded.

"That's when it happened. That night."

"Wow!"

She squinted her eyes. "So, you didn't know?"

"No! How would I?"

"You didn't even suspect?"

"No," I said a little quieter this time. I guess maybe in a way I had suspected something. Jax had been pressuring my girl, but I'd never really thought that Diamond had given in. We were only fifteen. I mean, it wasn't like I didn't know that lots of fifteen-year-olds were having plenty of sex. But not us; definitely not Diamond. Yeah, Diamond played all that fierce and fabulous stuff, but deep down, she was straight. I'd never thought she would have messed up like that.

"Aren't you gonna say anything?"

There was a lot I wanted to say, a lot I wanted to know. "So how, so what—"

"Girl," she said, waving her hand in the air, "it was like, whatever, whatever. It was no big thing really."

I couldn't believe she said that. I mean, having sex—that first time. That was major.

But then she got quiet. I could tell that she was thinking about it and that was making her all the way sad. "Have you ever had sex?"

I shook my head hard. "No, if I had, I would've told you. Why didn't you tell me?"

"It was so, so, so embarrassing. Remember, Jax stopped talking to me in school. That was right after I had sex with him, and that made me feel so bad. But my mom said it won't always be like that."

I knew I must've looked crazy with my eyes all wide. "The judge knows?"

"Uh-huh," she said, as if it was no big deal. "And so does my dad. And so does Pastor."

"Dang!" I screamed.

"I don't want to talk about this anymore," Diamond pouted. "Not until after you tell me your secret." The way she folded her arms, I could tell that Diamond wasn't going to let me get away with asking any more questions. But dang! My secret wasn't anywhere near as scandalous as hers.

"I'm going to find my dad."

She waited a moment before she said, "And?" like she just knew there had to be more..

"I'm going to find my dad," I repeated just to make sure she understood how big this was. "He's in New York, and I'm going to look until I find him."

Her eyes got a little wider; I guess my secret was sounding a little juicier, even though it still wasn't to her level.

I said, "No one knows about this. And I want you to help me *if* you can keep my secret."

"So, no one else knows?"

I shook my head. "I'm not even going to tell my mother, 'cause if I did, she wouldn't let me do it."

"And you don't know where he is?"

Again, I shook my head. "All I know is that he's somewhere in New York."

"So how are we going to find him?"

As soon as she said *"we,"* I knew my sistah was with me. "That's why I wanted to come here." I got off the bed and went to her desk.

Diamond followed me. "You're going to look for him on-line?"

"Uh-huh. I figure there must be someplace where we can put in his name and look him up."

"Are you sure he's in New York?"

"Yup. But if we don't find him that way, I already have a Plan B. I'll set up a personal page and start sending out messages."

"To who?"

"I'm not sure, but you know how everybody's always talking in school about meeting people on the internet? Well, someone in New York just might know something."

Diamond shook her head. "I can get with looking him up, but putting up a page? There're a lot of perverts out there."

"My sistah, *I know* all about perverts. You must've forgotten where I grew up."

"What does where you live have to do with this? The internet is just creepy. The judge won't even let me have a page. She doesn't want me chatting with a whole bunch of fools I don't know."

"We're not going to be chatting; we're going to be investigating. There's a big difference."

She sighed. "I'm not feelin' this, Vee."

"Look, I'm gonna follow all the rules. I'm not going to give out my phone number. I'm not going to meet anyone in person—you know, all that safety stuff everyone is always talking about."

Diamond was still shaking her head, but I needed her to be down with me. "If there's anyone who can peep a pervert, it's me. Haven't I been living with D'Wayne all of this time? And I'm still fine, right?"

She nodded.

"So you know I'll be safe and doubly safe because you'll be doing it with me."

It didn't look like my girl was going to budge.

With a sigh, I said, "Please, Diamond. This is super important to me. All I want is a chance to find my father."

That did it. "Okay," she said, turning on the computer. "What do we do first?"

I explained my whole plan as we waited for the computer to boot up. Then we went to Google. With a deep breath, I typed in my dad's name: Pierre Garrett.

I was on my way.

Chapter Nine

"Congratulations, ladies!" Sybil shouted as she and Turquoise came bouncing into the rec room with big ole grins on their faces. "I guess we're going to New York."

"Yeah," we said as they hugged each one of us.

We were all too excited. Practice didn't even begin for another fifteen minutes, but my sistahs and I had been hanging in the rec room at the church for almost half an hour already. Even Aaliyah, who was always complaining about wasting time, didn't mind just sitting around, talking about New York.

"Well, since we're all here, let's get started, and maybe we'll get out a little early."

I could tell by her smile that Sybil was as excited as we were when she sat down at the piano. All I wanted to know was what song we were gonna rock at the semifinals.

Diamond raised her hand like she was in school, but just like in class, she didn't wait for anyone to give her permission to speak. "Y'all need to know I'm not singing the lead."

Hold up, was what I said inside. Major shock. And by the

wide-eyed looks on India's and Aaliyah's faces, I could tell they couldn't believe it, either.

Diamond not wanting to have the spotlight? No way. Not with all the drama she'd brought last time about how we should all take turns singing the lead. That had just been code for her thinking there had been too much attention on me and not enough on her.

Looked like losing in San Francisco had made her step back.

"Okay," Sybil said slowly, like she was surprised, too. Then, she turned to me. "So, you're it, Vee."

If Diamond didn't want to be blamed for losing, what made Sybil think that I wanted that? I shook my head. "I don't want it, either."

Before Sybil could even look at her, Aaliyah said, "Don't ask me to sing a thing because—"

Sybil waved her hand in the air. "I know, I know." Then her eyes got small as she took her time looking at each one of us real slow, like she was trying to see through us or something. "What's going on here?"

Not one of us said a thing.

"Y'all are going to have to talk to me."

It still stayed quiet.

"I think I know what's going on," Turquoise said. She stood next to Sybil and crossed her arms. "This is about what happened in San Francisco, right?"

If my sistahs weren't giving anything up, neither was I.

Turquoise said, "You feel like you lost and you're scared that it's gonna happen again."

Well, that wasn't what I was thinking. I was thinking we were gonna win in New York. But just in case, I didn't want to be the one with the microphone in my hand.

"Let me remind you ladies what happened," Turquoise

kept going. "You won. Plain and simple. You won. Fair and square. The Faithful Five cheated, they were found out, the real winners were chosen. The Divine Divas are the state champions."

"Yeah, but . . . ," India began.

Turquoise interrupted, "There are no buts. Among the groups between the ages of thirteen and eighteen, you are the winners. So y'all need to forget about the way it happened and make up your minds that you're gonna do it again in New York!" She pumped her fist in the air like she was leading some kind of pep rally.

We were all quiet for a moment before Diamond said, "All I'm sayin' is that I don't want to be the lead."

Turquoise threw her hands in the air. I guess her pep talk didn't pep up a thing.

Aaliyah said, "I have an idea. Let's not have a lead and just sing together."

Now I was feeling that. "Yeah."

"I like that," India agreed.

Diamond said, "That's exactly what I was thinking."

But Sybil didn't like our idea. "This is your group, and I'll put it together whichever way you want, but . . ." She took a deep breath. "Vee and Aaliyah, your voices are amazing and should be showcased. You two are the weapons of the group."

Aaliyah crossed her arms.

Sybil held up her hand, stopping Aaliyah before she could even go into her I'm-not-singing-the-lead sermon. Aaliyah was my sistah, but even I was tired of hearing that song.

When Sybil looked at me, I said, "We're all good singers. We'll be okay just singing together."

"You've seen the other groups," Sybil said. "No one else does it this way."

"We're the Divine Divas," Diamond said as she held her

finger in the air. "We're fierce and we're fly. And we're not like other people anyway. Those other groups need to be afraid of us!"

India and I laughed, but Aaliyah just rolled her eyes.

"Well, at least I agree with you on one thing," Aaliyah said. "If we sing as a group, we'll win or lose together."

"That's right!" I added. "Together as sistahs."

Sybil looked at us for a long time before she shrugged. "If that's what you want, I'll make it work."

All of the excitement that Sybil had had just ten minutes ago was gone. She thought we were making a mistake, but inside I knew that only good things were going to happen in New York. Sybil would be feelin' it soon. We'd show her.

She flicked through the stack of sheet music on top of the piano. "Most of the songs that I picked out are designed for solos." She sighed. "I'm gonna need some time to come up with some choices, go over them with Turquoise, and we'll have it for you next week."

"Okay," we all said together.

"Before you guys go, I have an idea," Turquoise said. She motioned for us to sit down on the bench against the wall. "How would you guys feel about background dancers?"

"Other people dancing with us?" India asked.

Turquoise nodded. "Let's take those three minutes and turn them into a real production. That's what we did with the first show here in L.A. Remember how the audience was singing and dancing in the aisles?"

I remembered that for real—it wasn't supposed to have been part of the show, but on that stage, I'd been feelin' it. And I'd just started clapping my hands and yelling for the crowd to join us. Pretty soon, everyone had been out of their seats. And in the end, we'd won.

Turquoise said, "What you did in L.A. was entertain. But

we didn't do that in San Francisco. Let's do that again. I want to bring sexy all the way back," Turquoise said.

"Heeeyyy! Sexy! That's me! Sixteen and sexy. I'm feelin' that!" Diamond sang.

Turquoise smiled. "Then I'll put together a plan. Next week, I'll have something that will make it look like you ladies are singing at the Grammys."

"That's what I'm talking about," Diamond said, and we high-fived each other. Even Sybil was grinning again.

I was feeling crazy-good now. We had a plan to win as the Divine Divas, and I had a plan to win as Pierre Garrett's daughter.

There was nothing but victory in my future.

Chapter Ten

"Did you look at my page?" I asked Diamond the moment I walked into her bedroom.

She closed the door. We weren't alone in the house this time, although I didn't think their housekeeper, Carmen, was going to give us any trouble. Whenever I said hello to her, all Carmen did was smile.

"No, I didn't look at your page. Why would I do that?" Diamond answered. "This is your thing."

"I thought you would check on it for me—at least over the weekend." I moved right to the computer and clicked it on. After a minute, I signed onto the internet.

I was so excited, but when I looked over my shoulder, Diamond was sitting on her bed, texting somebody. As if finding my father was all about nothing.

I couldn't blame my sistah for not feelin' this like I was. I mean, she had her father; she couldn't understand.

My fingers were trembling as I opened my page. And then, I screamed.

"What?" Diamond jumped off her bed. With one hop, she was looking over my shoulder.

"I got messages!" I clicked on the message icon. Thirteen! I couldn't believe it.

Last week, after we hadn't been able to find a listing for Pierre Garrett in New York City, Diamond and I had designed my personal page. It had taken us two days, but I'd posted my picture and profile saying I was looking for my father—Pierre Garrett, who lived in New York.

"Should we put your dad's name on here?" Diamond had asked. "We don't want any imposters."

"No worries," I'd said, figuring I needed to play it straight. "I'll be able to spot a fake a mile away."

"How?"

I hadn't bothered to answer. And even though she hadn't been sure, I'd left my dad's name right up there. I would never be able to explain it to Diamond, but just like she knew her father, I would know mine. A fake would never get by me. Trust and know.

And now today, I had messages! Could one of these be from my father?

My hands were still shaking when I clicked on the first message—from Cool Hand Luke. Interesting name. Especially for a father.

"Hey," Diamond said the moment the message came on the screen. "He's hot."

I rolled my eyes. I didn't care not one single solitary bit what this guy looked like. And I cared even less when he talked about "hookin' up with a cutie like me." Not only was this boy not my father—could he even read? I hadn't said anything about hooking up.

"Yeah, he's a major cutie," Diamond said.

"Can we just focus, please?"

"I am!" She was telling the truth. She was focused, almost drooling over this guy's picture.

She dragged a chair over to the desk. "Let's see what else you got."

I should've been grateful to Cool Hand Luke. At least he made my sistah throw down her phone and give me some backup.

The next four messages were just like Luke's, from boys who wanted me to send more pictures, to the ones who wanted my digits. Then there were the ones who wanted to hook up in person. Like I would do something dumb like that.

I was getting pretty sick of it. But Diamond wasn't.

"Some of these boys are major cute," Diamond said. "Maybe I should make a page."

"I thought your mom wouldn't let you have one."

She waved her hand in the air. "When have you known me to listen to the judge?" Diamond asked. "And anyway, you have a page."

"I'm not her daughter."

"You think the judge is going to see the difference when she finds out about this?" Diamond laughed.

"She's not going to find out, right?" I said and clicked on another message. In two seconds flat, Diamond had stopped laughing. Both of our mouths were open wide as we read this one.

After awhile, Diamond said, "Eeewww! Gross! I told you this site was full of perverts!"

All I did was hit the Delete button. I didn't even want to think about the nasty things that guy had said. But a minute later, I was hitting the Delete button again. And then, again.

"See! I told you this wasn't going to work!"

I just kept deleting messages, trying really hard not to

listen to Diamond. But truth—she was right. All of those messages and not one of them had anything to do with my father.

Diamond pushed her chair back from the desk. "We need to forget about this," she said as I turned off the computer. "It's never going to work." She flopped onto her bed and grabbed her Sidekick again.

I was beginning to think that Diamond was so right. There weren't a lot of things that made me cry, but I felt like this was going to be one of those crying times.

"Let's talk to my dad," she suggested.

My eyes got all big. "No! I told you, this is a secret."

"Yeah, but searching the internet isn't going to work, and my dad can help."

Diamond didn't even know that she was making it worse. The first thing she did when she had a problem was turn to her father. Couldn't she figure out that I wanted the same thing?

"I don't want your father in this, Diamond. I want to do it myself."

"But—"

"Come on; this is just the first day. I have to learn how to really use the internet."

But it was like Diamond didn't even hear me. "Well, if you don't want to talk to my dad, what about Mr. Heber? Top Cop can find anybody!"

Okay, sure, Mr. Heber was deputy chief of police, but how did Diamond think talking to Aaliyah's father was any better? I didn't need to be reminded that they both had their dads. And India had hers, too.

I said, "Let's stick with this for a little while, *please*? And if it doesn't work, I'll figure something else out."

Diamond shook her head.

"We promised each other! This is my secret and you said—"

Diamond held up her hand. "Okay, okay. But . . ." She glared at me. "I'm not feelin' this."

"No worries. It's gonna work."

She sighed and grabbed her purse. "I hope so. You ready?"

I guess my sistah was ready to take me home. No prob—I was ready to go.

As I followed Diamond out of her bedroom, I was trying to figure out what I was going to do next. Because there was no way I was going to give up. Not now. Not ever.

Finding my father wasn't a choice; it was what I absolutely had to do.

Chapter Eleven

was loving this song.

Sybil had picked out "Everybody Get Up" and the beat was ridiculous. The words were mad-cool, too—all about getting up off your feet and praising God. I could see us rocking this all the way to New York.

Sybil hit the last chord of the song and we held the note for as long as we could. "Okay," she said, "that was pretty good for a first run-through."

My sistahs and I gave each other high fives. We were rocking it hard, kickin' the harmony, sounding way better than we'd sounded in L.A. and San Francisco.

"Now, don't get cocky," Sybil said. "We still have weeks of work ahead of us; y'all know that, right?"

"Yeah," we said together.

"Good. Now, take a look at the third stanza." Sybil took a deep breath. "What about each of you taking a solo—just one line each?"

I looked at India and Aaliyah, 'cause I knew my girl,

Diamond, was down for at least a one-line solo. I could tell by India's smile and Aaliyah's frown which way this was going. But before Aaliyah could go into her I-ain't-tryin'-to-sing-no-solo sermon, the rec room door busted open and Turquoise marched in.

"Ladies, are you ready to shine in New York?"

Not one of us said a word—all of our eyes were on the three boys who followed her.

"Hey, T," Diamond said, all sweet and soft.

"T"? Diamond had never called Turquoise "T." But one look at my sistah and I knew what was up. She was talking to "T," but she was staring at the guys, especially the one in the middle—the new boy in school, Arjay Lennox.

Turquoise dumped her bag on the floor. "Ladies, meet three of the best dancers in my all-male class I just started: Troy, Arjay, and Riley."

"What's up," all three boys said at the same time.

I kinda stood back and peeped this scene. It was hilarious, really. India was standing like a statue, while Aaliyah was staring the guys down.

And then there was Diamond, who was straight-up in her glory. She was smiling so hard, it looked like the corners of her lips were touching her ears.

The boys were playing it crazy-cool. They must've been friends, because they all stood the same way—side by side, with their thumbs hooked through the loops of their jeans. They looked like dancers.

Well, let me take that back. Troy kinda looked like a dancer. He was lean and long and looked a little like that old guy—Gregory Hines—who used to dance. And Riley—well, he may have looked a little like a dancer now, but it was hard for me to really see him like that because I never knew he danced. In school, all he ever did was study. I mean, he was the president of the math club. What kind of dancer loved math?

The one who really looked like a dancer was Arjay. He had long locks that hung loose to his shoulders. And with his black T-shirt, and that tiny earring (that glittered like a real diamond) in one ear, he looked like he could be holding it down as a dancer for Jay-Z or Chris Brown.

"Ladies, y'all look surprised." Turquoise laughed a little. "I told you I was bringing dancers."

"Yeah, but I've been thinking. Why do we need dancers?" Aaliyah asked, as if she didn't care that the guys were standing there. "This isn't a hip-hop contest."

I knew my girl was always straightforward, but I was a little surprised at Aaliyah. I mean, Turquoise had broken it down for us last week, and Aaliyah had been cool with it. But it seemed like she wasn't down with it anymore.

Turquoise was not fazed. "I talked this over with Pastor and Sybil." When she stopped, Sybil nodded. "We think this will add some flava to the Divine Divas."

"But that's just it," Aaliyah said. "We're the Divine *Divas*."

Turquoise waved her hands in the air. "Think Beyoncé, Christina, any of the hot singers. Even Zena!"

Although Zena was kinda old—like forty or something—she still rocked. Everyone loved her. She was Big Mama's favorite singer, and my mom played her CDs all the time. Everyone always said that Zena was like a young Diana Ross. I didn't really know a lot about Diana Ross, but I knew that Zena was hip, and so cool that she only had one name.

"Zena is hot!" Diamond said. "Did y'all see her open up the Grammys? She had like fifteen dancers on that stage with her, and they were *all* guys." She grinned. "I'm lovin' this, T," she said, looking Arjay up and down.

I rolled my eyes. Diamond was going all the way out for

this guy. I wasn't hatin', though, 'cause Arjay was fine.

"I think this is cool." Those were the first words India said since the guys had come in.

"Me, too," I said. If this was going to help us win, then I was down with it.

But Aaliyah still was not feelin' this. "I don't get it. This is a *singing* competition."

Diamond's eyes looked up to the ceiling, like she was saying a special prayer to God. "It is, and these guys are going to help us win. I thought you believed in winning."

"Hey!" Arjay held his hands up and then turned, like he was about to walk out the door. "If you guys don't want us . . ."

"No!" Diamond smiled at Arjay. "We want you." Then she glared at Aaliyah.

But that didn't mean anything to Aaliyah. She crisscrossed her arms and glared right back.

So I decided to try to help. "I think this is the kind of thing Glory 2 God is looking for, Aaliyah." I tried to speak to her soft, like I wasn't trying to force it. "They want a fresh group, and I think with the dancers, we can bring it."

Slowly Aaliyah nodded. "Well, if this is what it'll take . . ." She grabbed her bottle of water. "Ain't nothing but a thang for me."

Diamond was smiling again. "Hey, I'm Diamond," she said to Arjay, Troy, and Riley, as if she was meeting them for the first time. That was weird, because she knew all of them—at least a little bit—from school. But that was Diamond.

"What's up?" Arjay said. "So," he looked around at all of us, "everybody cool?"

India and I nodded. Aaliyah just kept sipping on her water.

Diamond said, "Everything is major cool."

Turquoise said, "Guys, can I talk to you for a moment?" She motioned for the boys to follow her to the other side of the room.

Diamond came over to me. "Isn't Arjay cute?"

I looked him up and down again. "Yeah, he's all right."

"What's wrong with *your* eyes?"

I laughed.

Diamond sighed, "I could just stare at him all day."

I didn't know if he was *that* fine.

"I think I'll call him 'The Face.'"

"Weren't you all crazy about Jax?"

"Jax who?"

I shook my head. "Whatever. Just stay focused, my sistah."

"Oh, I'm focused," she said, her eyes all on Arjay.

I sighed. There was nothing I could do about Diamond. All I would do was pray that this didn't turn into one big mess.

Chapter Twelve

I really need a cell phone, I thought as I ran up the stairs.
Then I would've called Big Mama and let her know that I
was gonna be late. It was only ten minutes after six, but still,
my grandmother hated when I wasn't there when she brought
my brothers home. Most of the time, she stayed with us until
Mama got off from work. But when she had something else to
do, all she wanted was to drop off D'Andre and 'em and be on
her way. I prayed this wasn't one of those drop-off-and-leave
times.

I was all the way out of breath by the time I got to our
apartment. I pushed the door open. "Hey, Big Mama."

"Your grandmother's not here."

I was shocked when I heard my mama's voice, and my
heart was pounding even more as I walked toward the
kitchen. Something big-time must've happened for my mother
to be home from work so early.

"Hey, Mama." I dropped my backpack on the floor and
waited to hear the bad news.

When she faced me with a smile, I breathed.

"Hey, baby." She pulled a pan filled with a big ole chicken out of the oven. "How was practice?"

I tried not to frown too much, but it was hard. My mother *never* asked anything about me. "Good." I was still trying to figure this out. The kitchen table was covered with all kinds of pots and bowls, like my mom was cooking a big holiday dinner. But Thanksgiving and Christmas were a long ways away. "Sybil kept us a little longer today because we met the new dancers."

"Dancers?"

"Yeah." I explained Turquoise's idea, but then went right back to trying to figure out what my mother was doing home on a workday. "Are you okay?"

"Yeah, baby." Mama laughed. "I just decided to take the day off; take a little time for myself."

Okay, so maybe nothing was wrong on the outside, but something was definitely wrong with Mama on the inside. Why had she been taking so much time off from work recently? In the two weeks since D'Wayne had been back, this was the third time Mama had taken off. Was she sick? Or maybe she was . . . no! I couldn't even think about her having another baby.

She said, "I thought it would be great to have a nice dinner. This'll be ready in a little while." She was so happy, it sounded like she was singing, when she was just talking.

I stared at her a little longer. She didn't look like she was pregnant. Now I was happy, too. "You want me to help with anything?"

"What about your homework?"

Oh, Mama was in a good mood, because she always wanted me to help, whether I had homework or not. "I have some words to study for French, but I can do that after dinner."

"Okay, make the salad. Wash your hands first."

I stood at the sink and listened as my mother hummed that new song from Zena, "It's Gonna Be All the Way Right."

The only time my mother was like this was on the days she got paid. That never lasted long, because after she paid the bills, she went right back to her tired-sad mood.

I loved hearing her hum. This was how I wanted her to be all the time. After I found my father, this would be her life. He would make so much money that Mama would never work again. She would stay home and cook and take care of us.

And she would never be tired. And never be sad. And would hum every day.

As I sliced up the tomatoes, I asked, "Mama, why did my father leave?"

She stopped humming, but she was still smiling as she stirred the rice in the pot. "Your father?"

I nodded.

"Are you asking because of what I said about D'Wayne and the boys the other day?"

I shook my head. Mama had no idea—I thought about my dad all the time. "I was just thinkin' . . ."

"Your father didn't just get up and walk out, baby. We both agreed to separate, because Pierre had other things he needed to do. He was dying to go to Europe."

Mama had told me that before. How my father wanted to hook up with his mother's side of the family.

She kept on, "He wanted to go to France, and I wanted to stay here."

"But he didn't stay there long, right?"

"Nope, he was back in like three months."

"So why didn't he come back here? Or why didn't you go to New York?"

"Because we both knew that we weren't supposed to be

together. We'd made a mistake. Pierre didn't love me. He only married me because . . ."

Mama stopped. Mama always stopped when she got to that part of the story. But even though she never said anything else, I knew the rest, because Big Mama had told me—Mama had been pregnant when she and my dad had gotten married. Big Mama had had to sign the papers because Mama had only been sixteen, the same age that Big Mama had been when she'd gotten pregnant with her baby—my mother.

That's why Big Mama was always telling me that I had to break the curse. And now that I was only a couple of months away from being sixteen, Big Mama repeated that story and her warning every single solitary chance she got.

I said, "I just wish he had come back to L.A. so that I could see him all the time."

"He didn't like Los Angeles, baby. He came here for college," she said, telling me the same story again. "But then we got married and had you. He had to work, go to school . . ." Mama's sad voice was back. "I know you miss him," she said softly. "But the way it turned out, it really was for the best."

How could my mother say that? The way we were living—this wasn't the best of anything.

Mama said, "Even though it didn't work out for your father and me, I always wanted you. I was happy I had you then, and I'm happy I have you now."

Mama always told me that. I think she never wanted me to feel bad. And truth—it did make me feel all the way good.

Then Mama said something that she'd never said before. "Your father wanted you, too."

At first I was shocked, but then I wondered, *Why am I surprised?* Of course my dad wanted me and loved me. He was probably looking for me right now.

"Do you ever think about Dad?" I asked.

" 'Dad'?" Her eyebrows went up high on her forehead, like she was surprised with the way I called him Dad. But that's who he was to me.

Mama said, "I don't think about him too much because it's been a long time since I heard anything from him. And for so many years, I've had D'Wayne." Her voice got all happy again.

Why did she have to go and mess up everything like that?

"D'Wayne has helped me move on," she said.

Move on? Move on to where? D'Wayne hadn't helped my mother do a single solitary thing.

It made me a little mad when Mama started humming again, this time that old song "Endless Love." As if she could only hum when she was thinking about D'Wayne.

But that was okay. Soon, she'd be humming for my daddy. I was going to make sure of it.

Chapter Thirteen

This wasn't working at all.

I looked over at Diamond, who was lying back on her bed, reading through her stack of magazines. In just a minute, I was going to have to tell her that she was right all along.

Turning back to the computer, I deleted the last message. There had been over thirty today. And just like the other ones I'd received over the last two weeks, they had all been silly letters from boys or some crazy emails from perverts.

What had made me think that I could find my father on the internet? This had to be the stupidest idea ever!

With a big ole sigh, I moved the mouse to log off, and then that soft bell rang, letting me know I had a new message. I didn't even want to read it, but what would it hurt? This would be the last one I'd read, and then I'd shut this down forever.

Hello. I'm Abigail Silver—owner of Child Find. I help kids
find parents esp n NYC. I can help u.

"Hey," I said, sitting straight up in the chair. "Look at this."

Diamond jumped from her bed, expecting to scope another picture of a cute boy. Standing behind me, she read the message aloud.

"How great is this?" I was all excited. "She can help me."

"How do you know she's not some kind of freak?"

"With a name like Abigail? She's probably just an old lady trying to do something good in the world. Look at her picture."

Diamond stared at the photo of the White lady who had a little smile and big silver-blue hair. "Well, let's make sure." Diamond pulled the other chair closer to the computer. "Ask her some questions. Find out how long she's been doing this."

I wasn't as suspicious as my sistah, but I guess it was good to check this out. So I typed the question, pressed Send, and waited. Not a minute later, a message came back.

10yrs. Ive found 100 parents.

"One hundred!" I didn't have any doubts now—she could help me. And she was in New York, too? This was like a gift from God.

But Diamond was not even moved. "Find out how much she charges."

Now that was a good question, because I didn't have a dime to pay. Abigail's message came back.

Im a non-profit. U dnt need $.

That was all right with me, but Diamond still had questions.

"Ask her how she does it."

I was so ready to send a message telling this lady to do her thing, but Diamond had some good questions.

Abigail wrote back.

Fathers who dnt c their kids have 2 report 2 the Child Services Agency. I have a list of millions of fathers.

"Wow," I said, after reading that message. "My father must be on that list."

"Definitely!" Diamond said, like she was a little impressed now. "I've never heard of the Child Services Agency."

"Why would you? Your father wouldn't have to register."

She paused for a second. "It sounds like she's cool, but I still think you should be careful."

As if she needed to tell me that. Diamond had lived in bougie Ladera Heights her whole life. I'd grown up in Compton. Which one of us knew how to be careful? I had more street sense in my finger than Diamond had in her whole body. Trust and know.

"Maybe we should research her company and that agency before you do anything else. We could ask my dad if—"

I didn't even let her finish. "I told you, I don't want anyone to know about this!" I was totally through with Diamond. Why was she trippin'? "You know what, if you don't want me to use your computer, I can just go to the library."

Diamond frowned. "I didn't say that."

"It just seems like you don't really want me to find my father."

"That is so not true! I just want you to be safe because of all the things that can happen online."

"All of that stuff happens with men, not women. Have you ever heard of a woman kidnapping a kid?" Before she could answer, I did: "No! Women are safe. And it's not like she's asking me for money, so what's the problem?"

I crossed my arms and waited for her to say something. Just one more thing about being careful and I was out!

She let a long moment go by. "Oh . . . kay," she said slowly. "You don't have to lose your mind. I was just sayin'."

Diamond was looking all sad and sorry; it was hard to stay mad. "I just want to find my father," I said softly.

"I know."

Just by looking at her, I could tell that for the first time, she got it.

"I got your back, girl," she said.

Truth—I knew that. No doubt, Diamond was my best sistah.

I hugged her. "I'm sorry. I'm just so excited 'cause this could be it. I could be close, and I want you to be excited with me."

"I am." She pulled her chair closer to the desk. "Okay, let's send Ms. Abigail an email. Tell her to do her thing. Find Pierre Garrett and find him quick!"

Chapter Fourteen

This was a special rehearsal. First of all, it was the first time we'd be practicing on a Saturday instead of the usual Monday and Thursdays—and it was the first time we'd be dancing with the guys.

For two weeks, we'd been singing and doing the steps by ourselves, then Turquoise would go off to her studio and do her thing with the guys. But today, we were putting it together.

"I'm really nervous." India's voice was quivering, like she was really scared. She tugged her T-shirt down over her leggings, trying to stretch it longer and cover herself up.

I didn't know why India was trippin'. I mean, yeah, she was on the shy side and usually wore big clothes to hide her body, but she was rocking those black yoga pants that Turquoise had told us to wear. She looked crazy-good in just about everything since she'd lost that weight. And truth—she looked better than all of us, 'cause she was the only one with some real booty.

"Why are you nervous?" Aaliyah asked her.

India shrugged. "I've never . . . like . . . not really danced with a guy before. I've just danced with you guys."

Sometimes I forgot just how different I was from India, how different I was from all my sistahs. They all lived in these big houses in nice neighborhoods, and I lived in an apartment in the center of Compton. They had relatives who lived in places like Beverly Hills, while my cousins Willie Lee and Bones lived in El Monte.

And whenever I went out to El Monte with Big Mama, I really remembered how different I was from my girls. Willie Lee was like eighteen and really smooth. And Bones was seventeen and a hustler. When I was with them and their friends, we'd listen to CDs and do the latest dances, hanging 'til after midnight on the steps in front of their house. Sometimes I'd even drink beer or sneak a smoke. Not that I liked that part, but I did it so they wouldn't call me School Girl. I did it to prove that I could hang, that I was straight-up cool.

But what we were doing today was nothing like hanging with Willie Lee and Bones. I couldn't figure out why India was scared to do a little dancing.

"Well," I started, "we aren't really going to be dancing *with* them. They're going to be dancing, and we're just going to be dancing *next* to them."

That didn't seem to help; India was still tugging and pulling on that shirt.

Aaliyah said, "Girl, you need to channel your inner Tova. You look so much like your mom now you need to start acting like her."

"Really?" India said.

"Yeah," I answered before Aaliyah could. "You know your mom would be all up in this."

That made India giggle a little.

"Where's Diamond?" Aaliyah asked.

I looked at my watch. I'd thought Diamond would've been the first one here—just waiting for the chance to get all up in Arjay's face, exactly the way she was at school. Every time she got a chance, Diamond was calling out to Arjay, waving to him, asking him questions in class, doing anything to get him to notice her. He always seemed nice enough, though not really interested. But that wasn't going to stop Diamond.

And right then, our girl busted into the rec room.

"The. Diva. Is. Here!" she announced.

She stood at the door with one hand on her hip, posing like she was some kind of movie star. And she was dressed that way, too. She had on leggings, but hers fit her more like they were part of her skin. And then she had on a little white top that barely covered her waist.

She had gone all Hollywood on us, with a black-and-white plaid scarf that covered her head and tied under her chin, and white Dolce & Gabbana sunglasses that were so huge they covered half her face.

"The diva is here!" she repeated. As if we hadn't heard her the first time.

She strolled across the floor, then stopped and whipped the scarf off. "We can start now."

India and I cracked up. Aaliyah was laughing so hard that she was rolling on the floor.

"Laugh if you want," Diamond said, not caring one bit what we thought, "but I'm a true diva, and y'all know it."

"You're a true something," Aaliyah said, still giggling. "What's up with this getup?"

"This," Diamond said as she swooped her hand down her side, "is what a diva wears. Because you know a diva always has to be on top of her game."

I didn't know if that was what a diva wore, but I did know that when Sybil caught a peek at Diamond, she was going to make her cover up quick.

I shook my head. "Like my mama always says, you're a hot mess."

"Whatever, whatever!" Diamond waved her hand in the air, dismissing me.

"Hey, ladies," Sybil greeted us when she came in. India, Aaliyah, and I were still laughing, so Sybil asked, "What's so funny?"

"You'll see," I said, then just stood back and waited. This wasn't going to take too long.

And it didn't.

Sybil took one look at Diamond and growled, "Where's your T-shirt?"

"What do you mean?" Diamond asked all innocently, looking down at the tiny baby-T she had on.

"What you're wearing is not a T-shirt. That's a hoochie-mama top."

We giggled, but that didn't faze Diamond. She shrugged. "Sorry, this is all I have."

Sybil's eyes got little when she crossed her arms. "You'd better find something else in your bag or you are on your way home."

Diamond rolled her eyes, even though I was sure that Sybil couldn't see since Diamond still had on those big ole sunglasses.

While Diamond dug in her bag, Turquoise arrived with the guys.

"Hey, everybody."

That made Diamond find another top, quick—a sweat-shirt. I could tell she wasn't happy when she slipped it over her head. But what did she expect? She had come to church dressed like she didn't have no sense. Sybil didn't play that.

Everyone kind of said hello to each other before Turquoise lined us up.

"Okay, let's make this happen. Ladies, I want the four of you up front, and guys, you'll be dancing behind them, in between each of the girls." It took only a couple of seconds to get set up. "Okay, let's do this thing. . . ." Turquoise frowned. "Diamond, what's up with the glasses?"

India, Aaliyah, and I giggled, and the guys just stared at her.

"Oh, I'm sorry," she said, slowly taking them off. "These are designer lenses that change with the light. It's so hard to remember when I have them on." She pushed them back over her hair, tucking them on top of her head.

Turquoise kept staring at her. "How are you going to dance like that?" She sounded like she was getting sick of Diamond. "Those glasses are going to fall off, and someone's going to break their neck."

"It better not be me," Troy whispered, loud enough for Diamond to hear.

When she turned around, he cracked his knuckles, like he was some kind of gangsta. But he gave her a big ole grin when she rolled her eyes.

It still took Diamond a while, like she just couldn't bear to be without her glasses. She got back in line, glanced over her shoulder, smiled at Arjay, and said to Turquoise, "We can get started now."

Turquoise had one of those looks on her face that my mother got sometimes, like, *Teenagers!*

She turned on the track. "Okay now, no singing. Just the steps. Get comfortable with each other, and then next week, we'll bring in the vocals."

The music blasted, and Turquoise raised her hands in the air. "Okay, now . . . one . . . two . . . three."

I dipped the way we had practiced and clapped my hands to the beat.

"More energy," Turquoise yelled. "Diamond, keep your eyes focused on me!"

It didn't take a great big imagination to know that Diamond was trying to dance and peep Arjay at the same time.

"Okay, that's good, go lower!" Turquoise kept on yelling. "More attitude."

I spun around and Arjay moved in between me and India. We held our poses while the guys came out in front and krumped. I had to admit, I was kind of impressed. I mean, something had told me that Arjay was going to be all that and beyond, but even though Troy was kind of tough and Riley was shy, the two of them moved like they were backup dancers for real.

"Veronique!" Turquoise yelled. "Keep up!"

I guess I had gotten off my game watching the guys, but it was hard not to notice them. Now Troy backed up against me, then he snaked around me to Aaliyah. And my sistahs and I kept dancin', and dippin', and kickin'.

I was so into it that even when the music stopped suddenly, I kept moving. It took me a moment to see Turquoise and Sybil standing with their arms folded, looking crazy-mad.

What had happened?

"Diamond! Arjay!"

Uh-oh. This sounded like big-time trouble.

With her hands on her hips and still huffing hard, Diamond said, "What's up?"

"What's up"? Oh, my sistah was acting out and showing off for real. Nobody talked to Sybil like that. I mean, she wasn't really old, just about my mother's age. But just like my mother, Sybil didn't play.

"What are you guys doing?" Sybil was talking, but her lips were hardly moving.

Diamond looked around, her eyes all wide, like she wanted one of her girls to help her out.

I turned around and looked the other way.

Diamond said all innocently, "I was just doing the steps the way we practiced and—"

Sybil held up her hand. "That is not the way we practiced!"

"I'm just trying to add some flava to my steps," Diamond grinned. "You know, keeping it real, keeping it hip."

Sybil looked at Arjay, and he held up his hands. "Hey, I was just following her lead. I figured this was her group—"

"This is not *her* group," Sybil said. She turned back to Diamond. "Nobody asked you to add nothin' to the steps!"

Okay, Ebonics coming out of Sybil's mouth? She was ticked off for real.

"You don't need to be dancing all up on Arjay like that. And Arjay—"

"My bad," he said before Sybil could finish.

Diamond shrugged. "Okay . . . if you don't want hip. . . ."

"I want hip," Sybil said, "and I want holy, too. I've told you that before—it doesn't have to be one without the other."

Turquoise clapped her hands. "Okay, we're gonna try this again. And like Sybil said"—she looked straight at Arjay and Diamond—"hip *and* holy."

I guess this time it was better, because we danced all the way through.

Turquoise changed a few steps, and by the time we did it for the fifth time, Sybil was back to smiling.

"Okay, that's a wrap. You guys did good."

We all clapped, and when Aaliyah dropped to the ground like she was exhausted, everyone laughed. I joined my sistah on the floor—we had worked hard for real!

"You guys can really do this dance thing," Diamond said, even though she was looking straight at Arjay.

"Yeah, I was a little surprised," Aaliyah said.

"And you were really hatin'," Troy said. "You didn't even want us to be part of this."

"It wasn't that. I just couldn't figure out how it was gonna work."

"Well, we worked it out," Riley answered Aaliyah, but he smiled at India.

Both Aaliyah and I peeped that before we looked at each other. Looked like our girl had a not-so-secret admirer.

Then Aaliyah asked, "Y'all wanna hang with us? We're going to Friday's."

Now that was a big surprise to me. I mean, we did plan on hanging this afternoon, but no one had said anything about the guys.

"Yeah, hang with us, Arjay," Diamond said, like he was the only one who had an invitation.

"That's cool. What about y'all?" he asked Troy and Riley.

Troy just shrugged, and Riley just smiled—at India.

I tossed my towel and water bottle in my bag. I was so glad that my mother had given me twenty dollars this morning, because I would have hated to miss out on this.

Seemed like some drama was coming for real.

Chapter Fifteen

We—all seven of us—squeezed into a booth that was made for about six. But no one seemed to mind. Especially not Riley, who was all up on India, and definitely not Diamond, who was practically sitting on Arjay's lap.

We placed our orders before Aaliyah asked, "So how did you guys become dancers?"

"My mom thought it would make me more outgoing," Riley said. "You know, I'm kinda shy."

He didn't look all that shy right about now.

I said, "Yeah, you always seemed that way in school, but you weren't shy today."

"Well, you know," Riley grinned, "I do what I do."

We all laughed, although India's was more like a giggle.

Aaliyah asked, "Do people ever think you're gay?"

Where did that come from? But that was my sistah; Aaliyah just spoke her mind.

"Dang, Aaliyah," Diamond said. She snuggled up closer to

Arjay, then put her hand over his. "You can just look at them and tell they're not gay."

"Why we gotta be gay?" Troy asked, all offended.

But Arjay wasn't even fazed. "Hold up, chief," he said to Troy. Then he turned to Aaliyah and said, "That's a good question." Arjay leaned back, stretched his arms along the top of the booth, and bobbed his head, like he was listening to music no one else could hear. "When I was younger, I didn't want to have anything to do with dancing. But now, all you have to do is look at Jay-Z and Kanye."

Troy added, "And Soulja Boy." Then, as if they had planned it, the three guys broke into "Crank Dat," singing Soulja Boy's song and moving as if they were on the dance floor. They were singing so loud that people at the other tables started staring at us. They were singing so loud they didn't hardly notice that we weren't feelin' them at all.

Before I could say a word, Aaliyah said, "That is so not the right song to sing here."

"Why? What's up?" Troy asked, even though he was still moving like he was dancing. "That beat is poppin'."

I took my turn to shut them down. "Have you *ever* listened to the words? It's so degrading to women it's not even funny."

"Degrading?" Troy laughed. "No, it's not."

Aaliyah said, "Yes, it is! It's offensive, and Black people need to listen to and think about what they're singing, rather than just going along because they like the beat."

Riley said, "Ah, you guys are just being sensitive."

"There's nothing sensitive about not wanting to be called a B," India said softly. "Or being called a ho." She kept talking, although we had to lean forward to hear her. "And every time some rapper calls a girl a ho, he's talking about your mother," she pointed to Troy, "and your grandmother," she pointed to Arjay, "and your sister!" she pointed at Riley.

That shut everybody down!

India never spoke up about anything, and I wanted to give her a standing ovation. My sistah was right on point.

Arjay twirled his glass of water in his hand. And Troy looked down at his cell phone.

Only Riley had the nerve to say something. "I guess I never really listened to the words. I mean, everyone just seemed to be singing the song and doing the dance, and I went along."

"Yeah, maybe we need to check out the words," Arjay said.

Troy looked at India. "True dat."

"Girl, you're somethin'; I like you." Arjay grinned at India.

"I do, too," Riley said. "I like you, a lot."

Okay, now!

The waiters covered our table with plates of hamburgers and fries and a salad for India.

Before I could take a bite, Arjay said, "Who's gonna bless the food?"

Riley raised his hand, and we all closed our eyes while he prayed.

Wow, this was something.

Just a couple of minutes ago, these guys were singing that awful song, and now they were praying. Try to figure that out!

It was quiet for awhile before Arjay said, "I like y'all."

"We like you, too, Arjay," Diamond said, as if she could speak for all of us.

I looked at Aaliyah, and together we rolled our eyes.

Arjay said, "So, y'all wanna hang out at a concert next weekend?"

Diamond dropped her burger onto her plate. "Yeah!" she screamed.

He laughed. "Don't you wanna know who's playin'?"

"Doesn't matter." Diamond was shaking her head so hard, I thought her ponytail was going to fall off.

"It matters to me," Aaliyah said. "It's not Soulja Boy, is it?"

"Girl, I ain't crazy." Arjay laughed. "Nah, this is Zena. My brother's one of her dancers, and they'll be in L.A. next Saturday."

Zena! That would be so cool. I'd never been to a concert before. Every time someone came to L.A., my mother never had any money for the tickets. And even though Diamond always offered to pay, my mother wasn't having it. So I always ended up staying home and hearing about it the next day.

But these tickets would be free. I hoped I would be able to talk my mother into letting me go.

Aaliyah frowned. "Zena's in L.A.?"

But before Arjay could answer her, Diamond said, "Your brother dances for Zena! Oh, my God! How hot is that?"

"Yeah, that's crazy-cool," I said. "Is that where you get your moves?"

"Nah, I got my own moves." Arjay gave me a long look, then grinned, and I wondered what that was about.

Diamond asked, "Are you sure your girlfriend won't mind you taking us to the concert?"

Okay, could my girl be any more obvious?

"I'm a free agent," Arjay said.

Riley said, "Me, too," as if we didn't know that.

"So, I'll see if I can get us tickets and even some backstage passes."

This was sounding pretty good to me and, from the way she was smiling, to India, too. And my best sistah, Diamond, was sold twenty minutes ago. But not Aaliyah. She folded her arms and pouted her lips—she was crazy-mad about something.

"So, anyway," Aaliyah said, "you guys don't have a problem dancing with a group called the Divine Divas?"

Now Aaliyah was the one who couldn't be more obvious. Why did she want to change the subject so bad?

Arjay got serious. "We were gonna talk to y'all 'bout that. There needs to be a name change."

No, he didn't! Change our name? Who did he think he was?

"Yeah, we can't be dancing for no divas." Troy cracked his knuckles.

I stared Troy down. If these guys got crazy up in here, I was ready. I would go Compton all over them.

"We were thinking that the name should be changed to the Three Ys Men!" Arjay said and then bumped knuckles with Troy and Riley.

"The Three Ys Men?" Diamond asked with attitude. It looked like my girl was ready to go off, too.

"Yeah, for Arjay, Troy, and Riley. Our names all end in Ys. Get it?"

I got it, but I wasn't gonna take it.

The guys busted out laughing.

"I'm just playin'." Arjay took a sip of his strawberry shake. "I don't care what the name of the group is. If y'all win, we win. Y'all become famous, and we'll be, too."

It took a couple of seconds before my sistahs and I laughed with them.

Arjay said, "But don't sleep on the Three Ys Men. Next year, you guys just might be our opening act."

Diamond laughed, but I didn't see a thing funny about that.

Arjay gave me another one of those long looks. "Come on, Vee. Lighten up. I was just playin'."

I took a sip of my soda and wondered why he kept looking at me like that. I turned and started talking to Aaliyah, but I could still feel Arjay's eyes on me, even though Diamond was all up in his ear.

What was this about? I wasn't sure, but I was so ready

to go. Not that I wasn't having a good time, but if Diamond caught Arjay looking at me like that, there would be crazy-drama. And I wasn't down for that.

I put my money on the table. "I gotta make a move."

"Okay! See ya!" Diamond said so fast that I wondered if she'd peeped Arjay staring at me.

"I'll walk you out," Arjay said as I scooted out of the booth.

"Nah, I'm cool. I'll catch y'all later." I almost ran out of that restaurant and didn't slow down until I was outside.

Arjay was cool and really, really was cute, just like Diamond said. But my sistah had made it clear he was hers.

And I wasn't going to get in the way of that. I planned on staying far away from Arjay Lennox.

Chapter Sixteen

This had been another miserable Saturday. After a great week at school and rehearsing with my sistahs and the guys, I was stuck at home—again—watching my brothers. Just thinking about today made me want to make my lie bigger—made me want to tell my mother that I had to work on Saturdays, too. But that would be some kind of a crazy risk. 'Cause then, Mama would probably call Pastor and tell her that I was working too much. And then . . . I didn't even want to think about what would happen. I just had to let it ride—it wasn't like I had to do this every Saturday.

Now, as if today hadn't been bad enough, I was in the living room watching *Beavis and Butt-Head*. At least D'Andre and 'em were quiet. D'Wight was already asleep, lying in my lap, and if this kept going my way, D'Andre, D'Angelo, and D'Marcus would be asleep soon, too. Then I'd be able to watch whatever I wanted to until Mama came home from work.

Right when I thought that, I heard Mama's key in the door.

Guess I shouldn't have gotten my hopes all high. Before I had a chance to wonder why she was home early, D'Wayne came stomping through the door by himself.

Oh, brother. Since he'd come back four weeks ago, he'd hardly been here when Mama hadn't been home. Which was all right with me.

Rolling my eyes, I went back to watching TV. I could feel him standing there, looking at us, but nobody said a word to him.

"D'Andre, your mama said it was okay to watch TV?"

D'Andre didn't say a word, and I didn't answer his stupid question either. Mama always let them watch TV. That's all we ever did in our house.

"Boy, you hear me talking to you?"

D'Andre said, "Yeah," but he still didn't look at his father. He just kept on half watching TV and half sleeping at the same time.

"Yeah, what?" D'Wayne yelled.

It wasn't like he was scaring anybody. None of my brothers moved.

D'Wayne just stood in the hallway, staring at us like he expected somebody to pay him some attention. When I couldn't stand it anymore, I stared right back at him.

He grinned, and then with a stupid little chuckle he went shuffling down the hall.

I shook my head and wished that he would disappear forever.

I was so glad when I heard the bedroom door close; I went right back to watching TV.

But that quiet didn't last very long.

"Lil' Mama!" D'Wayne called me from the back.

I told that fool that wasn't my name, and even though he called me over and over again, I didn't answer.

"Veronique!"

I guess he got the message. I shifted D'Wight off my lap and walked into the hallway.

"What?" I yelled back at him.

"Come here."

I walked slowly toward the bedroom. Before I stepped in, I said, "Yeah?"

"Come in here."

I stayed where I was and pushed the door with my foot until it was all the way open. And then, it was my mouth that was open wide. D'Wayne was standing there—almost naked. All he had on was his underwear, and he was grinning at me.

"Bring me a can of beer, Lil' Mama."

Like that was ever going to happen.

"Did you hear me?"

I guess I was still staring at him, because it took me a couple of seconds to say, "Get your own beer."

He laughed. "Do you like what you see, Lil' Mama?" He started moving closer to me.

That's when I got some sense and backed away from the room.

"What? You scared?"

Yeah, in a way I was. Because I couldn't figure out his game.

And then, Mama saved me.

The front door opened and, a second later, slammed.

"What y'all doing sleeping on the floor?" I heard Mama ask my brothers. "Where's Vee?"

"I dunno," D'Andre gave his regular answer to everything.

D'Wayne was gonna get it now, but when I turned back to the bedroom, I didn't see him. He'd run right into the bathroom.

I'm still gonna tell Mama, I thought as I ran into the living room.

"Hey, Mama."

"Hey, baby," she said with a tired sigh. She kissed the top of my head. But then her voice perked up when she asked, "Where's D'Wayne? He said he was going to get here before me tonight."

"Mama!"

But she was already halfway down the hall. "Sweetheart!" she called out before she stepped into their bedroom. "I got off early." I heard her mumble something else, and then the two of them laughed.

Now I didn't know what to do. I needed to tell her, but what would I say? If I told her what happened, D'Wayne would say he was only asking me to get him a can of beer. Knowing him, he'd probably turn the whole thing around to be my fault. Then Mama would be mad at me. And I'd get in trouble. And she might even pull me out of the Divine Divas. And then I'd never get to New York.

Okay—I wouldn't say a thing. It wasn't a big deal anyway. Nothing really happened.

But if he ever tried something like that again, it was gonna be all the way on!

Chapter Seventeen

This is what I printed out," Diamond whispered as she slid the paper across the lunch table. "It kinda creeped me out."

I couldn't wait to look at the chat log that Diamond had had with Mrs. Silver. She'd printed out the whole thing for me to read.

I had wanted to go to Diamond's house over the weekend, but even yesterday, I'd had to go straight home after church. Without any communication for two days, I didn't want Mrs. Silver to think I'd flaked out. So, I'd talked my sistah into getting online for me. It had taken a lot to get Diamond to do it.

"Why can't you just wait and talk to her tomorrow?" Diamond had whined as we'd walked out of church yesterday.

"Because it's been a couple of days and I don't want her to think I'm not interested."

"I'll get on and tell her you'll be back tomorrow."

"No!" I had shouted so loud, people in the parking lot had turned to look at me. I'd lowered my voice. "I don't want her to freak out. Remember how she keeps saying not to tell anyone? Just pretend you're me."

I'd had to talk and talk to Diamond until India had come out to find me because her parents had promised to take me home. And then later in the afternoon, Diamond had only done it while I'd stayed on the phone and told her everything to type.

Even though she'd complained, my girl had come through. She'd chatted, answered questions, and had printed out every word.

Now, as I was reading their conversation, Diamond said, "That lady still creeps me out."

I shook my head. If she thought Mrs. Silver was creepy, she should try living with D'Wayne for a minute. I was gonna tell my best sistah about what D'Wayne had done on Saturday, but if she was freaking out this much about Mrs. Silver, she'd lose her mind about D'Wayne in his underwear.

Diamond continued, "This lady asks way too many personal questions."

"She said she needed as much information as possible to get a correct match."

"But why does she need to know your measurements?" Diamond scrunched up her nose, totally disgusted by that.

That made me stop for a moment, just like I had stopped yesterday when Diamond had screamed after Mrs. Silver had typed that question. Truth—it had seemed kind of freaky to me, too. But I was just rolling with Mrs. Silver—the more she knew about me, the easier this would all be. Whatever information she needed to find my father I would give her. Trust and know.

"She needs everything she can get to help," was how I explained it to Diamond.

My girl shook her head. "I don't think . . ."

It must've been the way I stared her down that made her slow her roll.

"Whatever, whatever. This is your thing."

"Remember that," I said right before India and Aaliyah came to the table. I tucked the chat pages into my bag because I didn't want Top Cop, Jr. to see a thing.

"Remember what?" Aaliyah asked and looked at me as if she knew that I was up to something.

"Nothing," I said.

Just like her father, Aaliyah wasn't about to let it go. She turned to Diamond, and without saying a word, she started breaking my best sistah down.

Diamond's eyes got real big. "What? I'm not doing anything."

"I didn't say you were," Aaliyah said, twisting her neck as if she was some sistah-girl.

I laughed. Aaliyah was so far from that.

She pushed Diamond even more. "But you're acting like you're guilty." Aaliyah looked back at me. "Both of you." Her eyes got all tiny as she squinted.

As if she could scare me with that. She needed to step to me stronger than that. Her dad might have been Top Cop, but I lived with the Queen of Mean, okay?

But Diamond was a different story. All Aaliyah had to do was breathe on her and Diamond would break.

"I wasn't doing anything!" Diamond said over and over.

I was so glad when she finally stuffed her mouth with French fries. Because if she gave me up to Aaliyah, that would be the end. Aaliyah would get all up in my business and try to talk me out of this.

"Hey, y'all," Troy said as he passed by our table. He waved and kept right on moving. But Arjay and Riley stopped.

"Hey, Indy," Riley said.

"Indy"?

I said, "You see anybody else sitting here?"

Riley didn't even look at me. "Nope," he said before he squeezed between India and Aaliyah.

All I said was, "You go, India!"

Diamond scooted over. "You can sit right here, Arjay." That put him right across from me, staring in my face.

"So, what's up with y'all?"

I think Arjay was talking to all of us, but I wasn't sure, because he was staring straight at me.

Diamond answered. "Nothing, just hanging. Ready for practice?"

"Yeah." Arjay's locks swayed whenever he nodded his head. And he just kept looking at me.

"Well, you and Diamond better watch it today," Aaliyah said. "I'm getting tired of doing those steps over and over again because of you."

Even though we were all mad about it, we all laughed. During every practice, somewhere in the middle, Sybil would stop the track and Turquoise would yell at Diamond and Arjay.

"Girl, it's not just us. I see you over there putting on the moves," Arjay said to Aaliyah.

"Well, you know . . . I do what I do." Aaliyah put her hand over her mouth and giggled.

Okay, this was weird. I'd never seen Aaliyah act all crazy like . . . well, she was acting like Diamond. I shook my head. Arjay was the one who knew how to put on the moves—on everybody.

"Well, I'm with Aaliyah," I said. "Let's keep it cool in practice."

Diamond shrugged. "We can't help it if we have special chemistry, right, Arjay?" She hooked her arm through his.

"Right. Right." Arjay nodded. "Hey, I got some bad news for y'all." He said it like he was talking to everybody, but he was still looking at me. "Zena's L.A. tour dates have been canceled."

"Oh, no," Diamond said. "She never comes to L.A. What's that about?"

Arjay shrugged. "I dunno, but we won't get the chance to hang," he said, staring in my face. "I was looking forward to it."

It took me a moment to move my eyes away from him.

Diamond said, "Well, we can still hang, right? Maybe do something else."

He nodded. "True dat." He stood up, looked down at me. "I'll catch y'all later. You coming, Riley?"

"Nah," Riley said, staying right next to India.

"Okay. Holla."

Diamond pouted. "I'm so bummed about the concert." But then, just as fast, a smile came to her face. "But isn't Arjay so fine!" She didn't wait for me or Aaliyah to say anything. She peeped across the table at Riley and India. "Well, I guess India and I have the ones we want." She looked at me and Aaliyah. "Who's going to get Troy?"

Aaliyah and I raised our eyebrows at the same time.

"Who said I wanted any of them?" Aaliyah said.

Just as I was about to agree with my sistah, Arjay looked back at our table. Looked straight at me. Again. And this time, he winked.

I turned away quick.

"Yeah," I said, but my voice was kind of shaky. "Who said I wanted any of them? I'm just focused on school and the Divine Divas."

Diamond stood. "Well, we know which one is mine, right?" She lifted her tray from the table. "Holla," she said, then walked away.

"Later." I was sure Diamond was heading toward Arjay, and I worked hard to keep my eyes away from both of them.

But even though I didn't look, I could feel it—drama was coming my way.

♪ Chapter Eighteen

Oh, snap!

That's all I could say when we lined up in the rec room and Turquoise turned on the track. Just when we were about to pop that first move, Pastor Ford walked in. Even though I hadn't done anything, I still felt like I was cold busted.

My sistahs and the guys must've felt the same way, because Turquoise had to keep yelling, "More attitude," and "More energy," over and over.

We kept on dancing. Pastor kept on watching.

Today, Sybil and Turquoise didn't have to stop us one time. But they made us do our routine over and over for an hour.

Finally, Turquoise said, "Take five."

Take five? I needed more than five minutes; I wanted five days!

As we sat on the floor, resting and drinking water, Pastor Ford strolled over. "The Divine Divas . . . and guys . . . are looking good."

India was the only one who had the energy to say, "Thanks, Pastor."

The rest of us just kinda grunted.

Pastor Ford continued, "I'm pleased. And I think you guys are a great addition to the group." Then, she stopped and gave us one of those looks, like a big ole lecture was coming on.

"Now, there's one thing I want to say. While fame and fortune are wonderful . . ."

Oh, it was going to be one of *those* talks.

"It's important to remember why you're doing this. It's all to exalt God. Have fun—you're supposed to. But always keep your eyes on who you represent. You know what I say—sometimes the only Jesus some people may see, is the Jesus they see in you. Let's make sure that we're all the best examples we can be."

I knew what was up. Turquoise had brought Pastor in to shut us down. To make sure that this girl-guy dance thing was going to work—her way. Or, as she would say, God's way.

Pastor said, "Now with that said, can you guys run through this one more time?"

I didn't have enough in me, but who was gonna say no to Pastor?

It took us a while to get up, but when the track came on, we danced as if practice had just started. But in three minutes, we were done—for real.

This time, Pastor Ford, Turquoise, and Sybil clapped. I guess we'd done good!

"Okay, that's a wrap," Turquoise said. "We'll see y'all on Thursday."

Pastor Ford turned to me. "Vee, I want to talk to you. Can I give you a ride home?"

I nodded. "I have to pack up first."

"Take your time; meet me in my office."

Troy waited until we were by ourselves before he said, "Dang, girl, what did you do?"

"She didn't do anything," Diamond said, as if I needed someone to speak for me. "She's Pastor's pet."

"I am not." I rolled my eyes even though I wasn't really mad. I liked thinking that Pastor liked me best. "She wants to talk to me about some projects I said I'd help out with at church."

I hugged my sistahs and then yelled, "Peace" to the guys before I headed to Pastor's office. She was waiting for me, and together we walked to the side lot, where her Range Rover was parked.

"Where's Mary?" I asked about the driver who took Pastor everywhere.

"I sent her home because I was hoping you'd keep me company tonight."

Now, how was I going to keep Pastor company when she was the one driving me home? But I played along, and by the time we got in the car, I was talking and laughing, and forgetting all about her being my pastor. She felt more like a mom who I could really talk to.

"So, how's school? Have you done any more with that political team?"

"Not yet. I gave my ideas to the class president and he was feelin' them."

Pastor nodded. "And how are things at home?"

"I hate it there!" Those words came out before I had a chance to think about them.

Pastor Ford frowned. "What's going on?"

I had to bite my lip to stop myself from saying anything else. This was a hard decision—should I tell my pastor about what had happened with D'Wayne? If I did, Pastor Ford would probably say something to my mother, and then it would be on—but not in a good way.

Plus, I had hardly seen D'Wayne since that had happened. He was staying out of my way. I just needed to keep that stupid scene to myself.

"Veronique, you know you can talk to me, right?"

Pastor could probably tell that I was thinking hard. "Yeah." I took a deep breath and got my lie together. "It's just that I hate having to always take care of my brothers. Sometimes I can't do extra stuff at school or with my sistahs because I have to be home early."

I breathed when Pastor Ford nodded like she believed me. "I know you do a lot to help out," she said. "Your mother's blessed to have you, because she works very hard."

"Yeah, she does."

Pastor was quiet for a moment. "Maybe I can talk to your mother and—"

"No, Pastor," I said quickly. Talk about some crazy mess! Mama always said that what happened in our house had to stay in our house. "I'm fine with taking care of my brothers. And my grandmother takes care of them most of the time," I said. "Really . . . it's . . . not . . ." I couldn't believe I was still talking. I had already said too much.

Even though she was driving, Pastor was staring at me—maybe not with her eyes, but with her mind. Pastor just had a way of doing that. I prayed that she wouldn't be able to see everything that I was thinking.

Pastor said, "Okay. So, you know that political forum you suggested? I think I have a way to make it work at church. . . ."

I had never been happier to change a subject. As quickly as I could, I started talking about the ideas I had. Even though

I was talking, I was still thinking about all that other stuff in my head—especially about D'Wayne. And then, there was the stuff going on with Mrs. Silver and my father. I wanted to tell Pastor, but I just couldn't take the chance. When it came right down to it, I was totally on my own.

But I was cool with that. I could handle this. I could handle anything.

♪ Chapter Nineteen

Diamond was humming the tune to Timbaland's "The Way I Are," and just like I had asked her when she'd been listening to Soulja Boy, I wondered if she'd ever listened to the words to this song. Not that these lyrics were bad, but it was obvious my sistah didn't know what she was humming. Diamond was great and all, but she didn't have the heart for anybody who didn't have any money. Even though she would deny, deny, deny, she wasn't feeling any boy who didn't have deep pockets.

While Diamond drove, I read over the chat I'd just had with Mrs. Silver. Since Diamond had printed out the chat log for me on Monday, I'd started doing the same thing. It made me feel good to come home and read over all the things that me and Mrs. Silver talked about. It made me feel like I was getting closer to finding my dad.

I read through the messages we sent back and forth.

She wrote:

2 bad u can't come 2 NY whn I fnd ur dad.

I hadn't planned on saying anything yet, but I figured now was the time to tell her—since she'd asked.

I wrote:

im coming 2 NY

She wrote:

why ddn't u tell me? i'll find ur father by thn. Can u send me a few more pics.

I wrote:

Pics of me?

She wrote:

ys. im using photo-match. More pics will hlp. whn r u coming

I told her that I'd be there in two weeks and that I would send her new pictures in the next few days. I'd never heard of photo-match, but I planned on using Diamond's digital camera over the weekend.

"Earth to Vee."

I looked up. We were at my apartment already?

Diamond turned down the music. "I hope Mrs. Silver helps you."

"Really?" I said. All this time, I just thought Diamond was doing this because . . . well, I was making her.

"Don't you know that I've always got your back?" she asked.

"I guess, but I also know that you thought this was crazy-stupid."

"Not crazy-stupid." Diamond shook her head. "Crazy-scary. I mean, I don't like all that online stuff the way everybody else does. But this lady, she seems all right, like she's real."

I nodded. "She is, Diamond. She matched another girl with her father yesterday."

"That's so cool." Then Diamond bit her lip, and I knew what that meant.

"What?" I asked her.

"Are you doing this, looking for your father, because of D'Wayne?"

"No! It's because . . ." I stopped, not sure what to say. I mean, how could Diamond ever understand? Her life was so different. "Try to imagine not having *your* father, not ever even knowing him."

Diamond shook her head. "That's deep." She looked at me closer. "I never thought about it like that. Life without my dad? Shoot, I can't even imagine life without the judge." We both laughed at that, but then we got back to being serious quick. "I hope you find him," she said before she hugged me.

I don't know why, but that hug felt crazy-good, especially today. It was like one of my sistahs really got me.

"I'll call you," she said, then waved.

Standing on the sidewalk, I watched until Diamond turned the corner. There were times when I wished I could just go home with her and stay at her house forever. I wanted to live anywhere but here.

I kicked a soda can to the curb, plugged my earphones back in my ear, and stepped inside my building. There was so much noise—people shouting, radios blasting, TVs blaring—that I couldn't even hear my own music from my MP3.

When I got to my apartment, the noise was just as loud. My brothers were running back and forth in the living room, screaming, throwing their toys around like they had lost their minds.

What was going on? Big Mama didn't play that.

D'Marcus ran in front of me, almost knocking me over. D'Andre and D'Angelo were right there, chasing him, then they threw him on the couch. And in the middle of the floor, D'Wight was quietly playing with his trucks, like none of this madness was going on around him. Even though he was the only one acting like he had any sense, my baby brother still had a big problem—he was stinking like a skunk.

"Where's Big Mama?" I yelled.

D'Andre stopped screaming long enough to say, "She left."

What was up with that? Big Mama hadn't told me to come home early. "She left you here by yourself?"

D'Andre looked at me like I was stupid. "Nah, Daddy's watching us," he said, and he went right back to running and screaming.

Didn't seem to me like D'Wayne was doing any kind of watching.

I stepped over all the toys and picked D'Wight up. "Hey, boo."

He giggled as I carried him, but I wasn't laughing. I wanted to hold my nose, he was smelling so bad. The only good thing when I went into the hallway was that the door to Mama's bedroom was closed.

I changed D'Wight's pull-up, then put him right back in the middle of the living room. For a minute, I thought about cleaning up a little and making my brothers sit down and be quiet. But that's what D'Wayne was supposed to be doing.

I looked at the clock. This morning Mama told me that she was going to her other job when she finished at the hospital, which meant that she wouldn't be home for hours.

Soon I'd have to feed my brothers and get them ready for

bed. But I decided to let them yell until they got tired or got on D'Wayne's nerves. I didn't care which.

In my room, I sat at my keyboard, plugged in my headphones, thought about my dad, and started playing. It didn't take me long to come up with a melody.

Pastor Ford said that I had a gift. If I did, I got it from God . . . and my dad. My mother didn't care a thing about music.

I imagined my father sitting right next to me, the two of us making up songs together. We would do that all the time—we'd be a father-and-daughter duo singing everything—hip-hop, R&B, gospel, and probably even jazz, because that was probably the kind of music he liked. We could sing together and get a contract with a big label. I loved my sistahs, but I'd give them and the Divine Divas up in a minute to do that with my father.

I kept playing and singing, having a good ole time. So why did my brothers have to mess it up? I knew they were knocking on my door just to bug me. I ignored them, but they kept it up.

"Leave me alone!" I yelled out.

At least they didn't just barge in like they always did.

When they didn't stop, I stood up. Maybe if I yelled in their faces, they'd go away. But before I even opened the door, D'Wayne wobbled in.

"What do you want?" I growled.

"Why you being so nasty, Lil' Mama? I just wanna talk."

He almost knocked me over with his bad, beer-smelling breath. "I don't want to talk to you," I told him.

"You look good," he said as if he hadn't heard me. "You growing up real nice."

"What?"

"Yeah, pretty. Just like your mama." He put his hands on

my shoulders and then started pressing, like he was giving me a massage.

I knocked him away. "You'd better get up off of me," I said, backing up, not stopping until I hit the wall.

"Ah, Lil' Mama, don't be like that." He walked straight to me, and when I had nowhere else to go, he leaned forward, closed his eyes, and pushed his mouth right against mine.

"Eeewww!" I gagged and pushed him. But he didn't budge an inch. He was too heavy.

He kept pressing his lips on my face.

"Get. Off. Of. Me!"

He still wouldn't stop.

I tried to scream, but with the way he was leaning against me, I couldn't get any sound out. I pushed and pushed and still couldn't get away.

Then I remembered something I'd seen on *Oprah*. I lifted my leg and kneed D'Wayne right between his legs.

He screamed and dropped to the floor.

I ran out of there, through the hallway and into the living room.

D'Marcus yelled, "Where're you going?"

I didn't even stop to talk to my brothers. I just kept on running. Down the stairs. Out the building. Up the street. I didn't stop until I was standing in front of the liquor store on the corner. My chest hurt, and I was breathing so hard, I wondered if I was having a heart attack.

Bending over, I rested my hands on my knees. What just happened? Had D'Wayne really tried to kiss me?

I could not believe this.

All I wanted to do was kick D'Wayne's butt. But I wasn't going back into that apartment. Not without Mama.

But how was I supposed to get in touch with her? I didn't have any money. I didn't have a phone. I didn't even have my keys.

Then I remembered the telephone booth across the street. I dashed off the curb—right in front of an SUV. The brakes of the car screeched and the driver blasted his horn. I was on the other side when I heard him cursing at me.

But that didn't even faze me. All I was thinking about was calling my mother collect, and then she would make D'Wayne go away for good!

I lifted the receiver. No dial tone. Dang, now what was I going to do?

As I crossed back over, I heard, "Hey, Veronique, what's up?"

Three guys were standing in front of the liquor store. I'd seen them all before—almost every day. They were always in the same place, doing the same thing—just standing around talking, smoking, drinking.

One of them—the tall one with big and wild hair like mine and with two gold front teeth—hung out with my cousins Willie Lee and Bones whenever they came over.

"Hey." I slowed down as I walked over to them. I had an idea.

The real short guy said, "Oh, she's talking today."

I crossed my arms and looked him up and down. "I always talk."

"No, you don't." This time, it was the one who looked like a football player who had something to say. "You're always acting like you're stuck up. What's up with that?"

I rolled my eyes and turned to the one who knew my cousins. "I need a solid."

"Oh, so now you *can* speak," the real short one said.

"Come on, dawg," my cousin's friend said. "Cut her some slack." He grinned, and his gold teeth shined.

"Listen . . . ah . . . do you have a cell phone?" Even though they probably didn't have jobs, I figured they had cell phones.

"Don't you have a phone where you stay?"

I wasn't even talking to the short one, but he had to be the one to bring drama.

I waved my hand in the air. "Never mind."

Before I could even stomp away, my cousins' friend said, "He was just playin'. Here, use mine."

"Thanks." I grabbed the phone.

"What're you gonna give us for letting you use the phone?"

I wasn't using his phone, but the short one was still talking as if I was listening. I didn't answer, just turned around so they wouldn't hear me.

I dialed my mother's number; it went straight to voice mail.

"Mama!" I said, but then I stopped. It wasn't like I could leave her a message saying, *D'Wayne tried to kiss me.*

I clicked off the phone and wondered what I was supposed to do until she came home. I couldn't sit outside until midnight.

I started pressing the numbers for Diamond's cell, when the short one said, "Hey, I thought you said one call."

"It ain't your phone, dawg. Leave her alone."

On the first ring, Diamond picked up. "Who's this?"

"It's me, Vee."

"Vee? Where're you calling from?"

"I'm . . ." I don't know why, but my lip started trembling. "I'm outside—in front of my apartment. Can you come and get me?"

Even though I was trying to stay calm, I must've sounded frantic, because Diamond started yelling, "Are you okay? Are you okay?"

"Yeah, I'm cool."

"Okay, I'm home, so it's gonna take me about twenty to get there," she said real fast. "But I'll be there, Vee."

I clicked off the phone and said, "Thanks," handing the cell back to Gold-Tooth Guy.

"No prob. Tell Willie Lee and Bones to holla at me."

I nodded, pushed my hands into my jean pockets, and slowly walked back toward my apartment. When I got in front of the building, I looked up to the third floor. Our windows didn't face the street, but I still wondered what was going on up there. Were my brothers okay?

But I knew they'd be all right. D'Wayne wouldn't do anything to hurt them. He only wanted to hurt me.

I sat on the steps and watched the people moving in and out of the apartment buildings, going to their cars, or running to the corner bus stop. It was starting to get dark, and I was starting to get cold.

All of a sudden, the door behind me opened, and I jumped up. But it was only the Hispanic lady who lived next door to us. She almost stepped on me when she walked by, and she didn't even say, *"Excuse me."* That's just how it was in my neighborhood. Nobody talked to nobody.

But she had scared me. I couldn't take the chance of D'Wayne coming up behind me like that, so I moved to the side alley, in between the two buildings. And I waited. And I thought. And the more I waited and thought, the more scared I got.

All I wanted to do was cry.

I heard the screeching before I even saw the car. And then Diamond came around the corner on two tires like she was about to hurt somebody. When she stopped, I wanted to laugh. But I cried.

"Vee, what happened?" She pushed the door open for me.

I could hardly talk. "Let's . . . just go."

It wasn't until I was strapped into the front seat that I finally felt safe.

Diamond didn't say a word. She didn't even turn on her music. Just flipped open her cell. Right away I could tell she was talking to Aaliyah.

She told Aaliyah that there was trouble. "Meet me at my house," she said. Then, after some silence, she added, "Have your dad bring you and India, and I'll take you home."

I was so glad that Diamond didn't say anything else as she drove. She must've known that whatever had happened was serious, because she turned on some gospel music. I didn't even know she had that stuff on her MP3. But it felt good to hear the man singing about trusting the Lord.

When we stopped in Diamond's driveway, she took my hand and led me as if I couldn't find the way by myself.

"What are we gonna tell your mom?" I asked.

"The judge is at a convention; she won't be back til tomorrow, thank God. 'Cause you know she'd be all up in your grill. My dad's here, but don't worry. Just follow me."

Mr. Linden was sitting on the couch, reading a newspaper and puffing on a pipe. I didn't even want to bother him. Just wanted to stand there and stare. This is how a normal family lived.

"Hey, Daddy."

"There you are!" He looked up. "I wondered where you'd gone so fast." He smiled when he saw me. "Veronique! How are you, sweetheart?"

He called me sweetheart—like I was his daughter. I did everything I could not to start crying again. "Fine."

"So, what are you girls going to do tonight?"

"Practice. India and Aaliyah are coming over, too."

He laughed. "So, our house is going to be filled with the joyful sounds of the Divine Divas?"

"Something like that." Diamond kissed her dad, and I got one of those missing-feelings in my stomach. "When Aaliyah and India get here, can you tell them to come on up?"

"Will do." He went right back to reading and puffing, right back to being normal.

Inside her bedroom, Diamond threw her purse on the bed. "Tell me."

"I might as well wait until India and Aaliyah get here so I don't have to repeat it."

"Nuh-uh." She waved her finger in my face. "You're not gonna scare me like that and then make me wait. I'm not about—"

"Okay!" I held up my hands, knowing that she was never going to shut up. "It was D'Wayne. He tried"—I closed my eyes—"to kiss me!"

"D'Wayne the creep? Eeewww! Why did he do that?"

"I don't know. Because he's nasty?"

"Oh, my God." She turned toward the door.

"Where are you going?"

"To tell my dad. D'Wayne needs to be arrested!"

"No!" I grabbed her arm. "You can't say anything."

"Why not?"

"Because!"

She crossed her arms. "You're gonna have to give me something better than that. Doesn't your mother want him arrested?"

"I haven't told her. She's still at work."

Diamond marched back over to her bed, grabbed her cell, and pushed it in my face. "You better get to calling."

"What's up, y'all?" India asked as she walked into the bedroom right in front of Aaliyah.

Aaliyah didn't say a word; just marched over to me and stared in my face like she was looking for evidence or something. "What happened?"

127

Now I had to deal with *her* interrogation. "Well—"

Diamond didn't even let me finish.

"D'Wayne, the pervert, tried to kiss her, practically raped her, and now she won't tell my dad or her own mother!" Diamond said. If she hadn't been talking about my life, I would have started clapping, because that was some kind of dramatic performance.

"You were almost raped!" India screamed.

I had to cover her mouth. "No! Diamond's exaggerating. D'Wayne just tried to kiss me."

"Who's D'Wayne?" Aaliyah asked.

"The guy . . . her mother's boyfriend or whatever," Diamond said, waving her hands.

"Would everybody just calm down," Aaliyah said, "so that I can get the story straight."

I still had my hand over India's mouth. "Are you going to be quiet?"

She nodded, but her eyes were big, as if she was really scared. "India, he didn't hurt me."

"But," she said the moment I took my hand away, "he tried to rape you!"

"No! Not rape. He tried to kiss me."

"Well, to me, that's just as bad," Diamond said.

"It's not. And anyway, I got away."

"And what if you hadn't?" Diamond asked. "What do you think would've happened then?"

"I don't know."

"See!" Diamond threw up her hands. "Rape! Any time a grown man touches a girl, it's rape to me!"

Aaliyah stood with her arms folded, as if she was studying every word that we were saying. Slowly, she began nodding and reached for her phone.

"What are you doing?" This time, I was the one screaming.

"I'm calling my dad. He just dropped us off; he'll be back here in five minutes."

"That's right!" Diamond said. "That's even better than *my* dad. When Top Cop gets finished with D'Wayne, he'll be wishing he never put his lips on you."

I snatched the phone from Aaliyah.

She frowned.

"You can't call anyone. I haven't even told my mom yet and . . . I'm not sure that I should say anything to anybody."

"What?" It was like a chorus the way the three of them shouted at me.

At first, I'd been all about telling my mother. But now, with the way my sistahs were talking about the police and everything, I was scared. Suppose D'Wayne was arrested? And then got put in jail? There might even be a trial, and I would have to testify. And suppose the trial became so big that we couldn't go to New York for the contest?

I couldn't take that chance. I had to get to New York.

"Just listen." I waved my hands, trying to get them to calm down. "All he tried to do was kiss me."

"That's enough," Diamond said.

"And if I tell your father, Diamond, or your father, Aaliyah, and D'Wayne gets in trouble, my mom will be really mad."

"Yeah," Diamond said, "mad at him."

"But what if she gets mad at me?" I asked.

Aaliyah said, "Your mother's not going to be mad at you. Why would she?"

I looked into Aaliyah's eyes. And India's and Diamond's, too. They just didn't get it. They would never understand the rules of the hood—taking care of business, keeping your business your business, and staying out of other people's business.

"I just need time to think about this. Please, please, you can't say *anything* to *anybody.*"

My sistahs glared at me as if they couldn't believe what they were hearing.

"Remember," I said, "ride or die. Ride with me on this one."

The three of them mumbled words I couldn't understand, but I knew what they meant. They were on my side—no matter what.

I looked at my watch, and it was already after eight. My brothers had probably not even eaten. And suppose D'Wayne had walked out and left them alone?

I took a deep breath. "I gotta go back home."

"You can't go back there!" Diamond said.

"What time is your mom getting home?" India asked.

"Around midnight, but I'll be fine." I was trying to be strong, but I didn't feel brave at all. All I could hope was that the kick I'd given him would keep D'Wayne away. "I have to go home and take care of D'Andre and 'em."

"How are you going to take care of them if you can't take care of yourself?" Diamond demanded.

"D'Wayne won't try anything with my brothers there."

"Uh, duh? Every single one of your brothers was there before, and that didn't stop the pervert."

"But," I began, trying not to whine, "what else can I do about my brothers?"

Diamond said, "Well, if you're going, then I'm going with you."

"And what are you going to do?" I asked.

Diamond shrugged. "I'll spend the night. And if he tries anything, I'll be all up on him." She jumped around like she was doing some karate moves.

Diamond wasn't trying to be funny, but India, Aaliyah, and I still laughed.

"If you're on him like that, you'll both be in major trouble," Aaliyah said. "I'm going with y'all."

"Don't even think about leaving me out."

When India said that, I just wanted to cry. My sistahs had my back all the way. "I love y'all for wanting to do this, but on the real, you don't have to," I said.

Aaliyah asked, "Didn't you just say that you wanted us to ride with you? Well, we're riding. So, let's roll."

I watched as India and Aaliyah helped Diamond throw some jeans, a top, her pajamas, and other stuff into a small bag.

Not even five minutes passed before we were headed downstairs. Diamond told her father that they were spending the night at my house.

"Did you speak to your mother about this?"

"We just kinda decided. Please, Daddy."

I closed my eyes and prayed that he didn't ask too many more questions. My sistahs wouldn't give me up on purpose, but right now, they were on the edge. One more question from Mr. Linden and they might start telling all my business.

"Okay, you all are riding together?"

"Yes, Daddy." Diamond slung her bag over her shoulder and kissed him on his cheek. "I'll call you when we get there, and I'll be home first thing in the morning."

He walked us to the door and then watched as we piled into the car.

"Drive carefully," he yelled out. "And no talking on the phone. And no playing around in the car."

While India and Aaliyah sat in the back and called their parents from their cells, I didn't say a word. After they talked on the phone, my girls didn't say much either. I guess we were all just thinking about what would happen when we got to my apartment. Would D'Wayne try something? I didn't think he was that stupid.

And then there was my mother. What was she going to

say about Diamond, India, and Aaliyah spending the night? Would she know that something was up, since I hardly ever had my friends over?

"Can I use your phone?" I asked Diamond as we waited for India in front of her house.

"You're gonna tell your mom?"

"No, I'm just going to tell her about y'all staying over."

While we drove to Aaliyah's, I left my mother a message. And after I hung up, I closed my eyes and said a prayer that this whole thing was gonna work out right.

My sistahs were talking like they were brave, but I could tell they were kinda scared. Just like I was. But my reasons were different from theirs. Yeah, I didn't know what D'Wayne was going to do, but I was more worried about what my girls would think after they spent the night with me. I mean, all of them had been to my apartment before, but only Diamond had ever stayed over. How were we all going to stay in my tiny bedroom? And then, there was the bathroom situation. The one time Diamond had stayed with me, she'd almost freaked out when D'Andre had tried to get in the bathroom while she'd been in there. She couldn't believe that I had to share a bathroom with my brothers.

And what were we going to do for fun? It wasn't like I had a television or a computer or a playstation. . . .

This was not going to be good.

When we walked into the building, the same screaming people and blasting boom boxes that I always heard seemed louder with my sistahs behind me. And now I noticed something that I'd never paid attention to before—all the different smells of fish frying and tortillas cooking and red beans boiling.

I felt kinda embarrassed.

When I stood in front of the door to my apartment, though, all of those thoughts went away. My sistahs huddled around me, and the four of us just stared at the door.

"Do you have your key?" India whispered.

I shook my head. I had to take a big breath before I knocked on the door. Almost right away, D'Wayne opened it, like he'd been waiting for me.

"You . . ." Then he stopped when he realized I wasn't by myself.

Without taking my eyes off of him, I grabbed Diamond's hand and rushed inside, stepping over blocks, and trucks, and all kinds of toys. India and Aaliyah followed us.

I stopped in the middle of the living room. "Where're D'Andre and 'em?" I asked, still holding Diamond's hand. My girl was making me strong. All of my sistahs were—they stood there and stared D'Wayne down.

"Why you wanna know about your brothers?" he growled. "You just ran out of here and left them."

"You know why I left."

That made him back up. "They're in their bedroom. As if you care."

I wanted to tell him that I did care. I wanted to know if they had eaten and if they were okay. But I didn't want to push it, so I ran, with my girls, straight to my bedroom.

As if we'd all been holding our breath, we let out one big sigh.

"Okay," Diamond said, as if we had accomplished something major. "I don't think he'll come in here after us."

"Nah," I said, sure of that. "He'll leave us alone."

They all dropped their bags, then slowly walked around my bedroom like they were looking through a museum. The bad feelings I'd had came back. It wasn't like I had anything nice for them to see.

"Wow, your room is way, way cool," India said when she stopped in front of my keyboard.

"Yeah." Aaliyah was looking at my bookcase. "Look at these encyclopedias." She pulled one of the old books that Big Mama had given me from the shelves. "My dad told me that this was how he used to look up stuff when he was in school." She fell on the bed and started flipping through the pages. "He said we're totally spoiled by the internet."

"I think these pictures are mad cool," Diamond said, looking at the yellow-edged photos that were stuck on my wall.

This was crazy-weird to me. I couldn't imagine it, but it seemed my girls liked where I lived.

"Play something for us," Diamond said.

"Nah, I don't feel like it."

"But you have to." Diamond did her whining thing. "Because then we can dance. And dancing makes you brave!"

"Who told you that?" I asked.

"It's a scientific fact," she said. "Ask Aaliyah. She knows everything about anything that's scientific."

Aaliyah grinned. "Hey, if Diamond says it. . . ."

Since my sistahs had come here with me, I could at least do this. I sat down at the keyboard and hit the chords that started my favorite song.

"*Reaching for something in the distance,*" Diamond sang, holding my hairbrush in front of her mouth like it was a microphone.

"*So close you can almost taste it,*" India and Aaliyah joined in, holding their cell phones to their mouths.

We sang loud and we sang long. We sang that song until India collapsed on the floor. "Enough already. Please!"

Although I could've sung those words all night, I asked what else they wanted to hear.

"Oh, I know," Diamond squealed. "Can you play Zena's new song, 'Tornado'?"

"Yeah," I said. I liked that song, too. About how your life could be so out of control that you felt like you were in the middle of a tornado. Right about now, that was how I was feeling.

But while I played the melody, Aaliyah sat on the floor and went right back to looking at my encyclopedias, even though Diamond and India were jumping all around her.

When I had played it through one time, I stopped.

Diamond said, "Play it again!"

"Play something else," Aaliyah said, not even looking up from the book. "I hate Zena."

"Hate her?" Diamond frowned. "Why? She's mad cool."

Aaliyah finally looked up. "She is so not cool! She's old. Way too old to be singing those songs."

"Dang! Don't hate. And it's not like she's old-old. She's like our parents' age. And she makes major bank. Girl, you'd better recognize—Zena is who we want to be!"

Aaliyah slammed the book shut. "I don't want to be any-thing like her!"

"Dang!" Diamond held up her hands. "Okay."

"Hey, I have an idea," India, the peacemaker, said. She held up my box of Scrabble.

Aaliyah grabbed the box and said, "Yeah, let's play," al-though she didn't sound like she was in any kind of playin' mood.

But after about five minutes, we were having fun again.

I kept peeking at Aaliyah. Why did she hate Zena so much? She was always going off whenever anyone mentioned her name. It was crazy.

We'd been playing about an hour when someone knocked

on my door. I hoped it was one of my brothers, but I didn't think so. I hadn't heard a peep out of them since I'd come home.

We all got quiet, and slowly, I stood up. And my sistahs walked right behind me. I moved to the door, opened it, and then we all breathed.

"Hey, Mama." I hugged her as tight as I could. "I thought you were working late tonight."

"I put in a couple of hours." She kissed my forehead and then said, "Girls, how're you doing?"

"Fine."

Mama looked around the bedroom. "Did Vee offer you anything to eat or drink?"

My girls gave me up when they said together, "No."

Mama grinned. "What kind of hostess are you?" She kind of popped me on top of my head with her fingers, but I couldn't feel a thing through all of my hair. "Let me get you guys some snacks."

When my mother closed the door, Diamond whispered, "You're really not going to say anything?"

"Nope," I said, bouncing on my bed, totally relieved that my mother was home. "She's in a good mood, and I don't want to mess that up. And anyway, D'Wayne hasn't bothered us the whole time. He'll never try that again."

Aaliyah shook her head. "I've read a lot about guys like him," she said. "And he *will* do it again. Especially since he knows you won't say anything."

"How does he know that?"

"He's counting on it," she said, as if she knew all about stuff like this. "He knows you're kinda afraid of your mom."

"I'm not afraid of her."

But Aaliyah ignored me. "If you don't say anything this

time, he knows there's less of a chance you'll say something the next time."

"How do you know all of this?" Diamond crossed her arms.

"I've already told you, Diamond, there's a world of stuff out there in books that don't have pictures."

Diamond pouted. "What're you tryin' to say?"

"I'm sayin' what I'm sayin'. Stop trying to make this about you. This is about Vee telling her mom."

"Well, I'm with you on that." Diamond turned to me.

"Me, too," India added her two cents.

"Look," I said, already knowing that I wasn't going to say a single, solitary word. "D'Wayne's not going to try that again. Trust and know."

"And what if he does?" India asked.

"Well then . . . he'll just have to deal with my father."

That shut them all up—for a moment.

Aaliyah said, "Your father?"

"Uh-huh." I looked straight at Diamond and told her with my eyes not to say a word. If this story was going to come out, I wanted to tell it. "I'm looking for my father."

"Looking where?"

"I'm working with this lady who has a company," I said, leaving out the part about the internet. "She helps children find their parents—especially missing fathers."

"Is your father missing?" When we all looked at India like that was a stupid question, she added, "I mean, you don't talk much about him."

"He moved to New York when he and my mom broke up. But I think I can find him."

With the way Aaliyah was looking—as doubtful as Diamond had at first—I almost wished I hadn't said anything. But I wanted them to get it.

"I've missed having my dad around," I said quietly. Then I asked Aaliyah, "Haven't you missed your mother?"

It took Aaliyah a long moment to answer. "I was really little when my mother went away."

"'Went away'?" Diamond said. "That's a weird way to say it."

"That's mean, Diamond," India snapped.

Although I agreed with India, I understood what Diamond was saying. Aaliyah's mom hadn't gone away—she'd passed away when Aaliyah was just a baby. So Diamond was right—that was a strange way to say it.

India continued, "Maybe it's just easier for Aaliyah to say it that way."

"Hello?" Aaliyah waved her hand in the air. "I'm right here, ask me. You're right, India. It's easier . . . that way . . . because it's been hard without my mother."

"So, then you understand what I'm doing, right?" I asked. "If your mother was alive, wouldn't you try to find her?"

I wished I could've taken those words back, because it looked like Aaliyah was going to cry. "If my mother was alive," she said slowly, "I would try to find her . . . if I thought she loved me."

"Of course she would love you," Diamond said. "She's probably in heaven right now, loving you."

"Well, if I was sure of that, then I would look for her," Aaliyah said, "because everyone should be with the people they love."

"Ladies," my mother called before she came into the room with a tray filled with soda cans and bowls of chips, pretzels, and cookies. "Here you go."

While I helped my mom arrange the snacks and sodas on my desk, I thought about what Aaliyah had said—how everyone should be with the people they love. Wasn't that the truth?

That was just another sign to me to keep doing what I was doing.

I was going to find my father.

Chapter Twenty

I couldn't wait to be sixteen.

Then maybe I wouldn't be late getting to school almost every morning. Not that I had any kind of money to buy a car, but I had to do something to get off of that city bus.

I ran to my locker and was glad to see my sistahs still waiting for me.

"I was getting worried," India said.

"Yeah, the bus was late again."

"That's not why I was worried," India whispered.

And then I looked at Diamond and Aaliyah. All three of my girls were staring at me like they were in biology and I was a frog about to be dissected. "No worries, I'm okay."

"So, D'Wayne didn't try anything else?" This time, it was Diamond who was whispering.

"No, just like I told you last night," I said to Diamond. Then I turned to India and Aaliyah. "D'Wayne hasn't tried a thing. I've hardly even seen him."

Victoria Christopher Murray

That was the truth. D'Wayne had stayed out of my way the whole weekend.

From Saturday, when my sistahs had stayed with me most of the day, to Sunday, when they'd called me almost every single hour after church to make sure I was okay, I'd only seen D'Wayne last night when he'd come home.

"I told you guys," I slammed my locker, "D'Wayne ain't causing no more trouble. Trust and know."

They all looked like they didn't believe me.

"So, you made it through the weekend, that's easy enough," Aaliyah said. "Now what're you going to do after school until your mom gets home every night?"

"I got a plan for that, too," I said. "I told my grandmother that we're having a lot of practices for the Divine Divas, so I'm not going to go home until she's there."

"Maybe you should tell your grandmother what happened," Diamond said.

"Are you kidding? Do you know what Big Mama would do?"

"That's what I'm sayin'."

I shook my head at Diamond. There was no way I would tell Big Mama. If I thought my mother would trip, my grandmother would go all the way off.

"Look," I said, needing to come up with something that would shut down all this talk about telling someone. "We can't say anything to anybody, because if we did, it could turn into major drama. And that could get in the way of New York. . . ."

I left it right there. They loved me and everything, but on the real, not one of them was about to give up the Divine Divas and the NYC.

"So, what're you gonna do every day until you go home?" Aaliyah asked.

Before I could say a word, Diamond said, "You'll just hang out with me, at my house. And then you can finish your project."

"What project?" Aaliyah asked.

"Nothing," I answered as fast as I could. Although I had told India and Aaliyah about looking for my father, I didn't want them to know exactly how I was doing it. Aaliyah would shut me down for real. "Just some stuff for school."

Aaliyah twisted her lips, giving me one of those looks like she was my mother. Or like she was her father. "Uh-huh," she said, staring me down.

The bell rang three times, signaling the start of homeroom.

"It's a good thing I don't have time to figure out what you're up to," Aaliyah said, "but trust me—I will."

I played it off. "Who do you think you are? Top Cop?" I laughed.

"You better recognize! I'm not his daughter for nothin'!" She grinned before she and India walked off to their homeroom and Diamond and I dashed down the hall in the other direction.

Thank God for the bell, I thought, because if Aaliyah had had any more time, she would have pushed until she'd gotten my secret out of me. There was no way I could let her or anyone else know about Mrs. Silver, her company, and New York.

All of that had to stay on the down-low.

Chapter Twenty-one

I looked over my shoulder, and Diamond was on her bed again, just texting away.

"Who are you talking to now?" I asked.

"Arjay." She grinned. "I'm still trying to find out when we're going to hang out, but he won't answer me."

"He's not texting back?"

"Nah, he texts back, but he won't say anything about us hanging out."

"Well, maybe he's busy right now."

"Too busy to hang out with me?" Diamond said as if she couldn't imagine that. "Anyway, he just sent me a text saying he'll see me at practice tonight." She sighed and jumped up from the bed. "What's up with Mrs. Silver?"

"Just the same stuff. She asked me if I was really coming to New York, because she'll make sure she finds my dad by then."

"That's great, Vee!"

"Yeah."

Diamond frowned. "You don't seem so excited anymore."

"I am. It's just that she keeps asking me all kinds of weird questions."

Right then, the soft chime from the computer let me know that another message had come in. Diamond and I read it together:

Whts ur bra size?

"What!" I said.

Diamond's mouth was as wide open as mine.

"See what I mean!"

But before I could say anything else, another message came through:

If u lived n NY + we could meet n person, u would have filled out forms to get all this info. The more info I have the better.

I said, "She always says that she needs more information, but I don't know."

"Don't start freaking out now," Diamond said. "She's getting closer."

Another message came in:

OK thts all 4 now. Remember, dnt say anythng 2 any1 about ths.

I wrote back that I wouldn't say a word and that I had to log off.

"I really think she's going to be able to help you," Diamond said, as if she knew I needed to hear that. "She's on the computer every day, and she wouldn't be wasting her time like this for nothing."

I nodded, but I wasn't so sure anymore. This was a switch. For four weeks, I'd been trying to convince Diamond. But I was starting to wonder—like why did Mrs. Silver need to know my height and weight and measurements and shoe size and now, my bra size?

It seemed crazy to me. But maybe it wasn't as weird as I thought. Maybe she needed all of that for that photo-match program.

Maybe.

I clicked off the computer and tried to push every single solitary doubt I had away. It was probably the stuff that I'd been going through with D'Wayne that was freaking me out. Mrs. Silver was legit.

I had to keep believing that.

♪ Chapter Twenty-two

I sat on the floor, leaned back, and sipped from my bottle of water. I looked at my watch again. We were thirty minutes early. What was up with this? Diamond never liked to get anywhere—especially not church or practice—early.

Then Arjay busted into the room and I knew exactly what was up.

"Hey," he said to us. "What's going down?"

"Nothing." Diamond smiled. "We're just waiting for everyone to get here."

"I thought we were hooking up early to practice before Sybil and Turquoise came."

Diamond looked at me, and I rolled my eyes. But even though she'd lied big-time, I wasn't going to give my girl up.

She said, "I guess they all forgot. But we could practice." Then she gave me a look that meant this special rehearsal didn't include me.

Arjay sat on the floor right next to me. "If I got time to

chill, I'm gonna do that." He grinned at me, then motioned to my bottle of water.

"What?" I asked.

"Can I get a sip?"

I looked at my bottle and then back at Arjay. I didn't know him like that. But if he didn't mind drinking after me, that was on him.

I took a last sip of my water and was about to give him the bottle when Diamond said, "Here, you can have mine." She tossed him her bottle, then she crossed her legs and sat right in front of us.

"Thanks," Arjay said. "I rushed over when I got your text. Didn't have time to stop and grab a couple of bottles from the store."

"What were you doing?" Diamond asked. "Hanging with your boys?"

"Nah. I was at Hillary Clinton's headquarters with Maxine Waters's group stuffing envelopes."

"Really," I said. "You're for Hillary? I thought you'd be for Barack."

He shook his head. "I like the guy, but I'm not feelin' him for president. Not yet. He needs a few more years of experience."

"And what kind of experience does she have?" I said. "I mean, I didn't know being First Lady counted. And Barack will have great advisers, too."

He laughed. "So you're into this race?"

"All the way. I'm going to be working with Pastor on putting together a political panel for the people here at church."

"Really?" Arjay smiled and nodded like he was impressed. "You think I can get in on that with you? Help you and Pastor Ford?"

"Definitely."

"I don't get it," Diamond said.

I had almost forgotten that she was sitting there.

"What?" Arjay and I said together, then looked at each other and laughed.

Diamond was not laughing. "Why are you so interested when you can't even vote?"

"Man, we'd better be interested," Arjay said, as if he was about to give a speech. "These folks are making decisions that will affect *our* lives. This needs to be about us. We'd better be all up in it."

"I'm with you!" I said. "Because when I'm ready to go to college, I want to be able to go. And then, there's all that other stuff, like the war and gas prices—"

"You don't even have a car!" Diamond frowned, as if what I'd just said was crazy-stupid.

I wanted to smack her. I knew I didn't have a car. "Gas prices still affect me. And there're lots of other things for teenagers to be worried about, too."

"True dat." Arjay nodded.

"That's another reason why I like Barack," I said. "He's gotten everybody interested and he's brought the whole country together."

"But that's not enough for him to be running things. Now, I'm not saying my man is not good, he just needs some time in the game."

"Well, what about a Barack-Hillary ticket," I said.

"Or the other way around," he said.

We laughed, but Diamond sucked her teeth and stood up.

"Hey," Arjay said, "I would've thought you'd be all up in this. Isn't your dad Linden Winters?" he asked, sounding impressed.

"Yeah." She sighed, but she was smiling a little.

Arjay said, "He's like one of the best councilmen around."

Now Diamond was grinning. "He is, but since I can't do anything about gas prices and who's going to be president, I don't feel the need to talk about it."

"Well, what do you want to talk about?" he asked.

This was my sistah's chance, but she was blowing it. She just stood there, stuttering, "Well . . . we could . . . I mean . . ."

My girl didn't have nothing to say. She knew he wouldn't be into her designer labels and fashion magazines. After a couple of seconds, Diamond rolled her eyes and stomped away.

"What's up with her?" he asked me.

"She's just not into all of this. She likes other stuff, like what Gucci's new line is going to look like."

"That's pretty shallow."

"She's not shallow!" I said, trying not to get mad. "She's just interested in different stuff than you."

"But that kinda stuff doesn't make a difference."

"You can't say that." This time, I didn't even try to hide my attitude. It was one thing for *me* to talk about Diamond, but I wasn't going to let *him* diss her like that. "One day, she's going to be a big-time designer, and she'll have enough money to pay for someone's whole presidential campaign by herself!"

He laughed. "Okay, don't get upset. I'll give her her props. Especially since one day I might run for president and may need some of your girl's money."

I smiled; there was no way I could stay mad at him. But I still said, "You'd better pass on some respect."

This time when he laughed, I laughed with him.

"Do you really want to run for president someday?"

He shrugged. "I'm really interested in making our communities better. If I want to make a difference, I gotta get down with the government."

"That's so cool."

"What about you?"

I shook my head. "I don't want to run for office, but I want to make a difference, too. Especially with all the wars going on. People are always talking about finding a cure for cancer or AIDS, and that's cool, but I'd like to find a cure for war."

"Wow, I never heard anything like that before."

"That's because people think fighting is the solution to everything. There are so many wars going on in the Middle East, in Africa, in parts of Eastern Europe. That's killing a lot more people than some of these diseases. That's what we need to be up on."

"That's deep." He gave me a long look. "You know, you're pretty cool."

I grinned, then looked across the rec room at Diamond. She was sitting in the corner far away from us. It looked like she was texting someone, but I wasn't sure if she was doing that for real or just trying to ignore me and Arjay.

I didn't want her to be mad. I mean, it wasn't like I wanted any drama. Arjay was her man . . . at least she was trying to make him that. I wasn't about to get in the middle of this.

I pushed myself up, but Arjay grabbed my arm and pulled me back down. He did it so fast that I fell on top of him.

I giggled. "What're you doing?"

"Stay here. I like talking to you."

And then, I saw it—for the first time, I really saw what Diamond was talking about. The Face. With his brown eyes that were almost black, and bushy eyebrows. With his broad nose and lips that looked like he could really kiss. And then there was that dimple right in his chin.

I peeked at Diamond, and she was still texting. I just hoped she didn't hear what Arjay had said to me.

"Sit back down," he whispered. "Let's hang til it's time to practice."

"Okay," I said.

This time, when I looked over at Diamond, she was staring straight at me. *Uh-oh,* I thought. But there was nothing I could do. Arjay liked talking to me, and I liked talking to him.

So I just leaned back and stayed right there. I'd handle my girl later. I'd make it right with us, because I wasn't about to get caught up in any female drama.

Chapter Twenty-three

I was really late today.

I dashed into the building just as the school bell rang. I was sure none of my sistahs would be waiting for me, but when I got to my locker, Diamond was still there.

"Hey," I said, all out of breath.

"Hey."

I was a little surprised that she was smiling. I mean, it wasn't a big ole grin, but it was enough to let me know that she wasn't crazy-mad.

I wasn't sure how it was going to play out today, because last night, we'd sung and danced and rehearsed like we always did, but there had been a big difference—Diamond hadn't said a word to me . . . or Arjay. And she'd let everybody know that she wasn't talking to us by the way she turned her back whenever Arjay or I said anything.

Then, in case I had missed just how pissed she'd been, at the end of practice, she'd grabbed her bag, yelled, "Holla," and switched her hips right out the door without asking me if I'd wanted a ride, like she always did.

I wasn't too mad at my girl, though. First, she knew somebody else would take me home. And second, I knew she really liked Arjay. So I just needed to explain to her how it had gone down—how Arjay and I had been talking about politics—nothing else. But if she wanted me to stay away from him, then, as Aaliyah would say, it was nothin' but a thang. She wouldn't have to worry about me saying anything or getting anywhere near him ever again.

"Listen," we started at the same time.

We laughed, and she said, "Well, usually, I would let you go first."

"No, you wouldn't," I said.

She laughed some more. "Just listen, will you?"

"Okay, and then it's my turn."

Diamond held the stack of magazines in her hands closer to her chest. "I just wanted to let you know that I'm giving Arjay to you."

Huh? "What are you talking about?"

"I'm not interested in him anymore."

"And you think I am?"

"I *know* you are. And since I'm special like that, you can have him. Plus, it's not like he's all that interesting. He's too serious and really boring."

I couldn't do anything but laugh. "So, because you're special, you're giving me a guy who's boring and too serious?"

"Yup. And he's really not all that cute."

My eyebrows rose so high, they must've gone to the top of my head. "What happened to The Face?"

"I mean, he's all right. But can you imagine Arjay meeting my parents with all of those locks in his hair? The judge would have a fit. That's more your style," she said. "*Your* mom will love him."

It felt like there was an insult somewhere inside of those words, but whatever, Diamond didn't mean it. She was just being . . . Diamond.

"So, he's yours. My gift to you, 'cause that's just the way I are!" She grinned and walked off toward our homeroom.

As I stuffed some books into my locker, I shook my head. I guess this was just my sistah's way of letting me know there wouldn't be any unnecessary drama.

Well, good. Not that I wanted Arjay or anything. Yeah, he was cute and smart and I liked talking to him. But how could I get with Arjay? I mean, I was going to be sixteen in a couple of months.

Big Mama would have a fit!

Chapter Twenty-four

I pulled my earplugs out before I unlocked the door.

"Hey, Big Mama," I yelled the way I did every day.

But today there was no answer. And no sound of my brothers running around the place.

I looked at my watch. Just like I'd done this whole week, I called Big Mama about thirty minutes ago, and she said she'd be here by six. It was ten after now. I started toward my bedroom, then stopped. Suppose Big Mama had changed her plans and didn't have a way to reach me? Suppose D'Wayne came home and I ended up alone with him?

Since he'd tried to kiss me last week, he'd come home with Mama almost every night. Like he didn't want me to be alone with her. But suppose today he knew that I'd be here by myself? On the real, he could already be here, just waiting for me in my room.

My heart was pounding so hard, I could hardly breathe. Swinging my backpack over my shoulder, I dashed out the apartment and down the stairs, jumping two steps at a time.

Please, God, I kept thinking, *please help me.*

I was moving so fast that I bumped right into my grandmother as she came into the building with my brothers.

"Special, what's wrong with you?"

I was so glad to see her that I didn't know what to do. I threw my arms around her neck and hugged her tight. "Hey, Big Mama."

She leaned back and looked at me. "What's going on?"

"Nothing. I was just looking for you."

She gave me one of those looks like she didn't believe me as I took D'Wight from her arms.

My brothers were already a flight ahead of us. When they got to the third floor, D'Andre yelled out, "Ooohhh. Someone broke into our apartment!"

"What are you talking about, boy?" Big Mama asked.

When she and I came around the corner, both of us saw what D'Andre was talking about—I had run off and left the door wide open.

"Special," my grandmother said as she looked from the door to me and then back to the door, "did you leave the apartment like this?"

"I thought I had closed it," I said, following my brothers inside. "I just ran downstairs because I thought you were coming up and needed some help."

My grandmother's eyes got real small. "You don't ask me if I need help any other day. So, what's going on?"

"Nothing."

"Hmph." But even though she knew I was lying, she left it alone. At least for now. "Where's D'Wayne?"

It wasn't until she said his name that I realized that my heart was still beating like it was gonna break right through my chest.

"I don't know."

And then she said what she said every day when she brought D'Andre and 'em home. "Well, if God answers prayers, this will be the day when he won't come home at all." Big Mama didn't even care that my brothers were standing right there. She said to them, "Go change your clothes and I'll get dinner ready," like she hadn't just been dissing their father.

"You want me to help you, Big Mama?"

"What about your homework?"

"I don't have any," I lied. I did have geometry problems I had to solve, but I wanted to stay close to my grandmother. Even though D'Wayne wasn't here, I just felt safer that way.

"Put on a pot of water. I'm going to make some spaghetti."

As I got out the pot, Big Mama asked, "How's the Divine Divas?"

"We're great. The show's gonna be way better this time. I wish you could come to New York with us."

"Now if I do that, who's gonna watch your brothers?"

"I know. But I wish you could come, because even Pastor Ford says that we look real good."

"Well, maybe your mom can go."

Mama with me in New York when I found my dad? That would be crazy-cool. "D'Andre and 'em could stay with you if Mama went?"

"What do you think? It would be good for your mother to get away. Talk to her about it."

I put the pot down on the stove and kissed my grandmother's cheek. "Thanks, Big Mama."

She waved her hand in the air like it was no big deal. "I'd do anything for you, Special. So how's it coming along with those boy dancers?"

I don't know why, but I thought about Arjay when she asked that, and I couldn't stop grinning. "There's this one guy,

Arjay, who's the best. But he's more than just a dancer. He's all into politics and everything that I like. We like the same kind of music and movies. Arjay's real cool."

I looked up—and my grandmother was not smiling. I guess I'd said a little too much.

Big Mama said, "Remember, Special, the only way to keep the boy is to keep the boy waiting."

I don't know why my grandmother went all the way there. "I'm not thinking about Arjay like that."

"Hmmm ummm," she hummed like she didn't believe a word I was saying. "Your mother and I, we didn't keep them waiting."

I sighed on the inside. *Here we go.* I had to listen to this whole lecture again.

"But you're not going to be like us, right?" she asked. "You're gonna break the curse, right?"

"Yeah," I said slowly. But this time, I wasn't going to just leave it there—I had to ask her something that I'd always wanted to know. "Why do you call it a curse, Big Mama? Because if Mama had waited, then I wouldn't be here." My voice got softer when I asked, "Do you think I'm a curse?"

Big Mama dumped the spaghetti that was in her hand into the pot and ran over to me. Her eyes were filled with water like she was going to cry.

"Don't you ever think that, Special." She shook my shoulders. "You hear me?"

I nodded.

"You are *not* a curse. You're a special blessing from God."

"But you always say—"

"Forget about what I said. I'm just an old woman—"

"You're not old!"

"You're right." She gave me a small smile. "I'm a not-so-old woman who didn't use the right word. It's just that I want

162

you to be all that you can be. And a baby changes things. It changed a whole lotta things for your mama."

"But if my dad had stayed, it would have been better, right?"

"But you can't count on that. The boys, when these things happen, they never stay."

I had never thought of it that way. "So, my dad left because of me?"

My grandmother lifted my chin with her two fingers and made me look at her. "Not because of you. He left because of himself. He left because he wouldn't man-up and take care of his responsibilities."

"Mama said he left because they both wanted to break up."

"That's your mother's story, but the truth is if your father wanted to be here, he would be." Big Mama went back to the stove. "Why're we talking about him, anyway?"

I shrugged. "I was just wondering."

"No need to be wondering about him. You have so many wonderful things in your life. Keep your attention on school, the Divine Divas, good things like that."

I nodded like I agreed, but I knew she was wrong about my dad. He'd had a good reason for leaving, and if he could be here right now, he would be.

When I found my dad, everyone would see. He would explain what had happened for all of these years. He would tell everyone how he'd always wanted to be with me and how he'd always loved me. And then Big Mama would have to tell me and my dad that she was sorry.

I could hardly wait for that.

Like I did every night around eleven o'clock, I tiptoed into the living room to turn off the television that my mother and

D'Wayne always left on. But tonight, they were still lying together on the couch watching the news. At least that was better than *Beavis and Butt-Head*.

For a moment, I just stood there, looking at my mother and thinking about what Big Mama had said. I would do anything if Mama would go with me to New York.

I took a deep breath. "Mama." I pretended that D'Wayne wasn't even there.

"Yeah, baby?" My mother kept her eyes on the TV.

"Do you think you can come with me to New York? With the Divine Divas?"

Mama looked up and let out a long sigh. "I can't go to New York."

"Mama . . ."

"Don't start whining, Vee. You know I don't have New York money. And who's going to stay with your brothers if I go running off with you?"

"Big Mama said she would stay with them."

All the way across the room, I could see it in my mother's eyes—she was upset. "You talked to your grandmother before you talked to me? What did I tell you about our business?"

"I know, but Big Mama was asking me about the Divine Divas, and she thought it would be good if you went, too. And she said she'd keep D'Andre and 'em."

"She don't need to keep nobody, because I don't have New York money."

"Maybe we could ask . . ."

"I'm not asking anybody for anything," she said, her voice a little louder. "You need to just leave me alone about this. I'm tired." Mama took the TV remote and turned up the volume.

I couldn't believe she did that.

And then, it got worse. D'Wayne looked at me and grinned, like he was the winner and I was the loser. I stared at him, and he just kept right on grinning. All I could do was go back into my room.

I clicked off the light, and when I lay down, I felt like crying. But I wasn't going to do that. If that's the way Mama wanted it . . . fine! When I found my dad, I wasn't so sure that I would even come back here. With the way my mother was acting, why should I? It would be way better to just stay in New York and live with my father.

That's exactly what I was going to do.

♪ Chapter Twenty-five

"Oh, no!" Diamond yelled from her bed like something had gone big-time wrong.

I looked over my shoulder. My sistah was staring at a picture in one of her magazines. Rolling my eyes, I turned right back to the computer.

"Vee, you should see these pants. We need to be wearing *these* in New York."

"What're you talking about? Ms. Tova already showed us the designs for our dresses."

"But these pants—they're leather, and they're fierce!" She threw the magazine onto the floor. "Shoot!"

Truth—I loved my sistah. But on the real, why was she always so dramatic? And over a pair of pants! I couldn't handle her drama right now. Not while I was waiting for Mrs. Silver to come back online.

She'd asked me when I was coming to New York, and I'd reminded her that it was this weekend. Then all of a sudden, she'd told me to hold on, because she might have some news.

I was having a hard time waiting—what kind of news could she have? Could she . . . no! I didn't want to get my hopes up.

When the computer binged, letting me know that I had a new message, I started shaking.

Mrs. Silver:

> The call was 4 u. I have good news.

I held my breath.
Mrs. Silver:

> I found ur father.

I screamed.
Diamond jumped off her bed. "What?"
I couldn't even talk; I just pointed to the computer.
Diamond read the message out loud, and then she screamed, too.
My fingers were still trembling as I typed back:

> r u sure

Mrs. Silver:

> yes. Pierre Garrett brn n ny + he went 2 skl in LA. Im sure its him.

I wrote back:

> do u have hs #. Cn i tlk 2 him. whr is he.

Mrs. Silver:

hes n ny + looking 4wrd 2 mtg u. Ths weekend, rit?

I typed back that we'd be in New York on Friday afternoon.

Mrs. Silver:

heres a # 4 u 2 call on Sat morning. u MUST call @ ten sharp.

In my message, I typed:

i wnt 2 spk 2 my dad.

Mrs. Silver:

we'll come 2 ur hotel.

I frowned. Why did I have to wait until then?

Mrs. Silver:

rmber, dnt tell anyone yet. thts impt.

I wrote:

I won't.

Mrs. Silver:

ur dad cnt wait 2 meet u.

And then she logged off.

I just sat there, staring at the computer. Wishing there was more.

It was hard to believe—Mrs. Silver had done what she'd said she was going to do . . . she'd found my father. I couldn't believe the perfect timing, but she said she'd been working hard.

"Are you excited?" Diamond asked as I printed out the chat log.

I tried to come up with the right words. "I'm crazy-excited," I said. "Can you believe it? I'm going to meet my dad!" I didn't know if I wanted to laugh or cry.

"Yay!" She cheered and gave me a high five. "And, it's great that they'll be coming to the hotel. That'll be safe."

I frowned. "I'm not afraid of my father."

"I know." Then she grinned and hugged me. "This is so great. So," she said as she bounced on the bed, "what do you think he's like?" She was talking all fast.

I sat next to her and shook my head. "I don't know."

"Well," Diamond began. Her hands were moving in the air with her words. "You know he'll love music, because that's where you get your talent from." Diamond stated that as a fact.

I nodded.

"He probably plays the keyboard," she added.

"And maybe even something else, like the trumpet or saxophone."

"Or maybe he's totally cool—maybe he's a drummer!"

I laughed. "That would be crazy-cool."

"And you know, he loves all things political. He might be like the mayor or something."

"The mayor in New York is an old White guy. He is definitely not my father!"

"I know." Diamond laughed. "I'm just imagining." She put her finger on her chin like she was thinking. "Oh, here's something. He probably has a big ole afro."

We laughed together. Diamond was coming up with all kinds of neat stuff. In just a few days, we'd find out for sure if she was right.

Diamond said, "This is so . . . so . . ."

"Fabulous!"

She laughed and added, "And fierce!"

"And cool!" I said. "Crazy-cool!"

♪ Chapter Twenty-six

W e're gonna do this one more time," Sybil shouted.
All of us moaned.

"Okay," Sybil chuckled. "Look at it this way, ladies and gentlemen—this is the final rehearsal before we get on a plane to New York!"

We cheered and gave each other high fives, but when I stood in front of Arjay, he didn't give me a high five; he hugged me.

"All right!" Sybil called out as she clapped her hands. "From the top."

Turquoise shouted, "And I want to see everything you got!"

I took my place and a deep breath. I was still feeling kinda dizzy from Mrs. Silver's news yesterday.

Stay focused, I said to myself as the track came on. I didn't need to be thinking of anything except for this song.

"Everybody Get Up," we sang in perfect harmony.

And then Diamond, India, Aaliyah, and I marched to the

front of the make-believe stage, strutting with attitude, like we were really divas.

"Send the praises up," we sang and twisted our backs to where the crowd would be.

We sang and the guys danced. They krumped and then weaved all through us, just like we had practiced together for six weeks.

"Then the blessings will flow," I sang while Arjay wiggled in front of me. It took everything in me to keep my eyes off of him.

We sang the last chorus and the guys came in front and did an old-school break dance that Arjay had come up with last week. Then we came around front and dipped in front of them.

We held that pose for five seconds. Nobody could tell me anything; we'd nailed it.

Turquoise and Sybil jumped up, clapping. And then we heard another voice.

"That was wonderful!" Pastor Ford said, applauding as she came through the side door. "You ladies . . . and gentlemen make me very proud."

We were out of breath, but it didn't stop us from grinning like we had already won the competition. I knew we had a long way to go, because any of the groups who made it to New York were going to bring it when they got on that stage. But I wasn't worried—we were gonna shut the whole thing down!

"Well, I'm not going to keep you any longer," Sybil said. "Go home, start getting your minds ready for New York. We'll have a chance for one rehearsal in New York, and then . . . it'll be on."

This time when they clapped, we did, too. And we all hugged.

When Arjay came to me, he whispered, "Hey, I'm driving tonight; you need a ride?"

Out of everything that had ever happened to me in my whole life, there was not a single solitary thing that had ever surprised me more.

"Uh . . ."

"No worries," he said. "I just thought I could give you a ride and maybe we could hang out a little . . . before I took you home."

"Uh . . ."

"I mean, if you don't want to—"

"No! I mean, yes! But I can't. I gotta do something with Diamond." But then, real fast, I said, "Maybe we can hang next time."

He grinned. "Yeah, in New York."

I had this stupefied look on my face and had to get away from him real fast or else I might never stop grinning. "Okay . . ." And then I ran away from him like somebody was chasing me down.

Diamond was all the way on the other side of the room, and I grabbed her arm.

"Ouch!" she yelled.

But I kept pulling her along.

"What . . . are . . . you . . . doing?" She stumbled beside me.

I didn't say a word until we were outside. "I had to get out of there."

"What happened?"

"Arjay."

From the look on her face—a half smile and half frown—I wasn't sure if she wanted to hear what I had to say or not.

But when she said, "Girl, you better tell me," I did.

"He asked me out. He wanted to give me a ride home and hang tonight."

"Really?"

"Yeah." Then I asked, "Are you okay with that?"

"I gave him to you, didn't I?" she smirked.

"Yeah, you did." I grinned.

"So, are you going to ride with him?" she asked. "Don't worry about me, 'cause—"

"No!"

She frowned. "Why not? Don't you like him?"

"No. I mean, maybe, I don't know. But . . ." I stopped. How could I tell her that I didn't want Arjay to see where I lived? At least not yet. I didn't want the first thing he found out about me to be that I lived in Compton. Not when he lived in Beverly Hills. "I have to get home 'cause . . ." I didn't even have a good lie. It wasn't like Big Mama was waiting for me. She knew this was the last rehearsal, and she'd told me to take my time getting home.

"Can you just take me home, please?"

"But why . . ." Diamond stopped, crisscrossed her arms, and leaned back as if she needed to get a better look at me. "Girl, do I need to school you on boys or something?"

I rolled my eyes. Like Diamond could teach me anything about that. She might have had sex first, but I was still the one with the street smarts. "I have to get home, and I don't want to be sidetracked."

"Whatever, whatever."

When she moved toward the parking lot, I ran down the stairs behind her, feeling like I was going to explode with excitement. We were on our way to New York. I was on my way to meeting my dad. And now, Arjay wanted to hang with me.

I never thought I would ever say this, but my life was so good. And as good as it was now, it was about to get one million percent better!

Chapter Twenty-seven

I was still feeling great when I ran up the stairs. I couldn't wait to tell Big Mama about our rehearsal. I busted into the apartment; Big Mama wasn't there. Neither were my brothers.

But D'Wayne was. He was standing in front of me, right in the middle of the living room.

I didn't give him a chance to say anything; I turned around and ran out of there.

"Lil' Mama," he yelled before I got to the stairs. "You don't have to go. I'm leaving."

That was the first time I really looked at him; I frowned. What was he doing wearing a suit? I'd never seen him dressed up before. It wasn't like I would ever believe anything he had to say, but it did look like he was going out.

"You don't have to run away," he said, following me into the hall. "Like I said, I'm outta here."

I glared at him but didn't move from where I was standing. I pressed against the wall, right in front of the stairs so that I could make a quick getaway if he made a stupid move. If he came anywhere near me, I would scream until Jesus came down from heaven.

Slowly, D'Wayne walked with his hands in the air like he was being arrested . . . and then he moved past me, turned to the stairs, and didn't look back.

I watched him walk down to the second floor. And even when I couldn't see him anymore, I listened for his steps to make sure that he was not coming back.

Then I ran back into the apartment and locked the door. Just a little while ago, I'd been feeling so good, but now my heart was beating so hard.

Where was Big Mama? It was almost seven, and she said she'd be here by six.

I grabbed the telephone and dialed Big Mama's cell. It went straight to voice mail. Okay, that probably meant that Big Mama and D'Andre and 'em were on their way. Maybe she had stopped to get my brothers something to eat.

Right then, I heard the key jingling in the lock. Thank God! I ran to the door, swung it open, and stared right into D'Wayne's face.

"Thanks, Lil' Mama."

He walked into the apartment, and my first thought was to get out. But he blocked my way.

He slammed the door closed, then started moving toward me. I backed up, not taking my eyes off of him.

I wanted to ask why he had come back. What did he want? But the look on his face—his eyes all wide and his mouth in a big grin—stopped me from saying anything.

"I forgot to tell you something, Lil' Mama."

It was hard to talk, because it felt like there were big ole rocks in my throat. But I was still able to squeak out, "What?"

"Your grandmother called," he said, dropping his keys on the kitchen table.

Just a minute ago, my heart had been beating so hard that it had hurt. But now it didn't feel like my heart was beating at all.

"She's keeping the boys at her house tonight," he sneered. "Some kind of emergency with her neighbor. . . ." He waved his hand in the air like he couldn't remember the rest of the message.

"So, it's just you and me, Lil' Mama."

I wished to God that I had told Big Mama what D'Wayne had done before, because she would've never given him that message. She would've never left me alone with him. But I hadn't said a word, and now I was sorry. Now I was in big trouble.

"You better leave me alone," I said as loud as I could.

"What?" he said when I was against the wall and didn't have anywhere else to go. "You think anybody's going to hear you? Everybody's always screaming in this building."

I was really scared, but I tried not to show it. "You'd better leave me alone," I repeated.

"And if I don't, what're you going to do? Kick me?" Then he started talking through his teeth. "You try that again and I'll break your legs." He was standing so close, his breath was all in my face.

"You better get away from me!" I was shaking real hard, but I wasn't going to just let him kiss me.

"What you gonna do, Lil' Mama?" And before I could say anything, he answered his own question. "Nothing. Because we're alone." He pressed his legs against mine, holding me in place. "So, what you gonna do?" he whispered.

I tried to push him away, but his body didn't budge.

"Get away from me!" I had held them back, but now the tears came. "Stop!" I screamed.

He put his mouth over mine. I started to gag when he

pushed his tongue in my mouth. Now I couldn't even scream.

But that didn't stop me from pushing and pushing.

He pulled his mouth away and started licking my neck. And his hands moved, all over my body.

"Get away from me!" I screamed.

He laughed.

And his hands kept moving.

And I kept pushing.

And he kept laughing.

And then it all stopped.

"What! Is! Going! On!"

Both of us jumped, and D'Wayne backed off. I ran straight to my mother.

"Mama!" I was crying so hard, I couldn't say another word.

But I wish I had, because D'Wayne said, "Baby, I'm so glad you're here. I'm telling you, you're going to have to watch this one. I couldn't believe what she was trying to do with her fast self."

My mouth opened so wide, but I still couldn't talk. I could hardly breathe. "Mama . . . he . . . was—"

"Don't listen to her, Lena."

I said, "He was . . . kissing me. And . . . touching me."

"You lying little . . . ." He stopped, smiled at my mother. "Baby, you know how she is. She struts around here and stuff. I came home and she was all over me. Telling me that she wanted to know what it was like to get with a man."

"Mama," I cried.

"I should've told you this," D'Wayne continued, "but she's tried this before."

"Mama!" was all I could say.

"Yeah, she's come onto me a couple of times. But I didn't tell you because I didn't want to hurt you, baby."

I was shaking my head so hard, but no words came out of

my mouth. With the way my mother was staring at me, I had to say something.

I wanted to tell her the truth, but it was hard to talk and cry. "Mama, I didn't . . . do . . . that."

She just kept staring and staring at me, not saying a word. Finally, she said, "D'Wayne?"

"Yeah, baby?"

"Get your . . ." My mother was shaking when she turned to him. "Get out of my house!" she screamed.

"Baby!"

"Get out!" I had never heard my mother yell so loud. Not even when she was screaming at me and my brothers.

"Come on, after all we've been through," D'Wayne said. "You're going to believe her over me?"

"I said . . ." Now my mother's voice was low. And her lips were hardly moving. "Get out of my house before I call the police!"

"The police?" D'Wayne acted like he was in shock. Then he put this stupid little grin on his face. "Baby, come on. This is me." He punched his fists against his chest.

"Veronique, get me the phone." Mama's voice was shaking, and she didn't take her eyes off of him.

His smile was all the way gone now. But he still kept standing there.

I handed her the receiver, and the way Mama walked right into D'Wayne's face, I thought she was going to hit him upside his head with the telephone.

She growled, "I'm giving you one more chance to just walk away. Because if I have to call the police, you better pray that they get here quick."

She just kept staring into his face until she looked down and started dialing.

That got him moving. "Okay!" He held up his hands. "I'm

out." He moved toward the door. "But you're gonna be sorry when you find out which one of us is telling the truth. Hit me on my cell when you get some sense." He didn't even look back when he walked into the hallway.

Mama walked behind him and locked the door. She stood there for a moment before she came to me. "Are you okay?"

I nodded, but I was still crying.

She put her arms around me. "What did he do to you, Vee?"

I shook my head. "Nothing."

"Are you sure? 'Cause if he did, you don't have to be afraid. You can tell me anything, everything."

"He just tried to . . . kiss me."

"Okay."

"And touched me."

My mother's eyes got real small. "Oh, baby."

"But he didn't hurt me. You came almost right away."

She nodded.

"Mama, I'm not lying."

She hugged me tighter, and I could feel her shaking. "I know you're not," she said, and we sat on the sofa together.

"I didn't know . . ."

"I know," my mother said in a soft voice. She held me until I stopped crying. It felt like almost an hour passed before she asked, "Do you want to talk about it?"

I shook my head. There was nothing more to say. D'Wayne was gone and I was sure he wouldn't come back this time. He was probably too afraid that I was up here right now telling Mama about all the other times. And then she'd call the police for real.

My mother nodded. "Okay, let me go change my clothes. Are you gonna be all right?"

I nodded.

"I'll fix us something for dinner," she said.

"D'Wayne said D'Andre and 'em are staying with Big Mama?"

"They are."

"Then I'll fix something, Mama. For you and me."

My mother smiled at me with her lips. But not with her eyes. There was so much sad stuff in her eyes that it scared me.

"I'll be right back," Mama said.

She moved slowly. Like her whole body was sad.

I watched my mother walk until she went into her bedroom and closed the door. I knew what happened with D'Wayne was not my fault.

But that didn't stop me from feeling really bad.

Chapter Twenty-eight

This would have been a good morning to stay in bed and sleep late, since my brothers weren't home. But all night I had turned over and over, thinking about how I'd had the best and the worst all wrapped up in the same day. It had been hard to sleep last night, with New York and Arjay and Mrs. Silver and my dad . . . and D'Wayne . . . all in my mind.

And now that the morning light was in my room, I wanted to get up and get back all the excitement I'd had from Monday and Tuesday—before D'Wayne had done all that nasty stuff. But it was hard to be happy when I thought about Mama.

Last night, she hadn't even come out of her bedroom. Even when I'd knocked on her door and told her that I had baked some chicken wings, she'd stayed in her bed.

"I'm not hungry, baby," was what she'd said to me. She hadn't even looked up. Just lain there and stared at the wall.

I had wrapped up the chicken. After seeing Mama, I hadn't wanted to eat anything either. Then I'd gone into the bathroom and taken the longest shower ever!

But now my stomach was growling. I put on my bathrobe and was shocked when I went into the kitchen. Not only was Mama already up, but she was dressed, sipping her coffee and staring out the window.

"Morning, Mama."

She smiled, but just like last night, her eyes were sad. And now they were wet, like she was a minute away from crying.

"Morning, baby. You gonna get something to eat?"

"Uh-huh," I said. But I didn't move. All I wanted to do was hug my mother and tell her everything was going to be all right. Didn't she know that she didn't need D'Wayne?

Mama waved her hand at me. "Get something to eat, Vee," she said. "Don't want you to be late for school."

I nodded even though I had plenty of time. It wasn't even seven o'clock yet. I pulled down a box of cereal, then got the milk from the refrigerator. But I wasn't so hungry anymore.

I watched my mother stare out the window, and I knew how I could make her smile. I wanted to tell her so bad. I wanted to say, *"Mama, don't be sad, because Daddy's coming home."*

But I couldn't. I had to play this exactly the way Mrs. Silver wanted.

"A locksmith's going to be here this afternoon."

"What?" I'd gone into my own dream world and didn't have a clue what my mother was talking about.

"To change the locks. Can you come straight home from school?"

I wasn't really feelin' that. I mean, I didn't think D'Wayne would come back, but I couldn't be totally sure.

Mama must've read my mind, because she said, "D'Wayne won't be here," as if she *was* sure. "He didn't take his keys"— she pointed to the keychain on the table—"but I want the locks changed anyway."

"I'll be here, Mama."

She nodded, eyes still sad. "And Big Mama's gonna be here, too. I'm gonna pick up your brothers today."

Boy, D'Wayne had changed everybody's schedules around. I said, "Does Big Mama . . . know?"

Mama nodded. "She wanted to come over last night, but I told her we were fine."

"We *are* going to be fine, Mama."

Her eyes looked like she didn't believe me.

Mama yawned. "I have a long day ahead of me." I hated that she sounded tired already.

I watched as Mama went inside her bedroom and sat on her bed. She stared at the wall again before she slipped on her shoes.

"Vee," my mother said when she came back into the living room, "do you want to . . . talk to someone?"

I didn't have a single, solitary clue what she was talking about.

Mama put her hand on my shoulder. "Do you want to talk to someone? Pastor Ford, a doctor . . . about what happened?"

I shook my head. "Mama, I'm fine. Really. I promise." I didn't know another way to say it. I really was fine. Now that D'Wayne was gone and Mrs. Silver had done her thing, I knew we would all be better than okay.

"I just want to make sure." A moment passed, and then Mama said, "I'm sorry."

I frowned a little. "You didn't do anything."

She nodded. "Yes, I did. I brought D'Wayne into this house. I let him stay." Holding my face in her hands, she said, "If he had hurt you . . . oh, God!" Her voice was choked up.

I gave my mother a hug. "Mama, please don't be sad."

She held me tight, then kissed my cheek. "I'll see you later," she said and patted my hair.

When she got to the door, she turned back and gave me a little wave, with her eyes still so sad.

I wanted to cry when she closed the door, but I wouldn't, because I already knew that everything was going to be all right. In just a few days, my mother would have happy eyes again.

Chapter Twenty-nine

I hadn't had a chance to tell my girls what had happened, since the bus had made me late for school again and then I'd missed lunch to go to a Rock the Vote presentation. But now we were all at our lockers, and my sistahs were huddled around me like they were protecting me.

"I cannot believe you're just telling me this!" Diamond whispered, as if she didn't want anyone else to hear us. "Why didn't you call me!"

"Because it was late and there was nothing you could do anyway."

"I would've done something," Diamond said.

"You should've called me!" Aaliyah said. "I would've been right there with my father, and D'Wayne would've gotten what he deserved."

That would have been some mad mess—the police at my house. I don't know if that would have been better—or worse.

I shook my head. "This played out exactly the way it was supposed to," I said. "And now, D'Wayne's gone."

"Your mom must've been really upset," India said. "My mother would've gone crazy."

"Yeah," Diamond said. "Drama Mama would have gone all the way off. But can you imagine the judge? Right now, D'Wayne would be up under the jail."

"Well, the Queen was really mad," I said, remembering the look on my mother's face. "She didn't even listen to his lies. She just told him to get out or she was gonna call the police."

Diamond said, "I would've thought your mother would've beat him down or something."

"I think she wanted to, but she was staying sane because I was there."

"Well, he got off easy," Aaliyah said.

I nodded. It did seem like D'Wayne was getting away with this. But on the real, could someone go to jail just for kissing somebody? "All I know is that I'm glad he's gone so that my mother can go on with her life."

"Yeah," Aaliyah said. "Especially if you find your dad."

I almost fell over. I couldn't believe she was bringing up my father right now, right when I was going to meet him in two days.

"What's up with that?" India asked. "Is that lady still helping you?"

I gave Diamond a quick look before I said, "Nah, that wasn't working out. But I'm not gonna give up."

India said, "Wouldn't it have been great if you could have hooked up with him while we were in New York?"

The way Diamond bit her lip, I knew she was on the verge of saying something. She moved her feet back and forth like she had to go to the bathroom. For all her drama, she should've been a better liar.

I said, "Yeah, that would've been cool, but I know God will help me find him."

"I know that's right," Aaliyah said.

I felt kinda bad bringing God into my lie, but I'd apologize to Him and my girls when this was all over.

"Well, let's all hang at my house till your mom gets home," Diamond said.

"Nah, I gotta go. My mom's having the locks changed."

"Boy, this is serious. Want me to go with you?" Diamond asked.

"Yeah," India said. "We'll all hang so you won't be by yourself."

I grinned. These were my girls. My sistahs—ride or die.

"Don't worry, Big Mama's gonna be there, so if D'Wayne is stupid enough to show up, he'll be sorry."

We all laughed a little. I guess we had the same picture in our minds of Big Mama beating D'Wayne. 'Cause she wasn't like Mama; she wouldn't have cared if I was standing there or not.

"Anyway, why are we talking about that loser?" I slammed my locker. "I mean, today's our last day. We're on our way to—"

Before I could finish, a guy yelled out, "Hey, Divas. Good luck in New York!"

Grinning, we said, "Thanks," all together.

I turned back to my girls. "That's what I'm talkin' about. Y'all need to go home and get ready for tomorrow. You know, it takes time to be a diva!"

Diamond laughed. "You got that right, and I need my beauty sleep, 'cause I've got to be fierce and fabulous in the NYC."

Aaliyah rolled her eyes, but India and I laughed as we moved toward the doors. More kids stepped up to us, wishing us good luck and lots of blessings. Through the crowd, I kept looking for Arjay. I hadn't seen him, Troy, or Riley all day.

Diamond asked, "Want a ride?" bringing my attention back to my sistahs.

"Thanks," I said before we did a group hug. "The next time we see each other, we'll be on our way to New York."

"Yeah!" my sistahs said.

"We're the Divine Divas!" Diamond yelled.

The kids around us cheered, as if we were stars on Broadway or something.

"We're in it to win it," Aaliyah said, twisting her neck with attitude. "And everyone in New York better recognize." She snapped her fingers three times.

My sistahs and I were ready to go shut down the NYC!

Chapter Thirty

I stuffed my last pair of jeans into the bag and clicked the locks shut. I couldn't stop smiling when I looked at the new suitcase Big Mama had bought me.

"You're always spoiling that child," Mama had said to her mother when she'd come home with D'Andre and 'em this afternoon and I'd shown her the camouflage duffel bag with wheels. But I could tell that Mama hadn't been mad.

"Special is my girl," Big Mama had said. "And she's a diva. She's got to go to New York in style. You can bet those other girls will have lots of new stuff."

See, my grandmother got it. Now I could get on the plane feeling as good as my sistahs.

I clicked off the light and got under the covers. I should've been asleep by now. It was almost ten, and our plane was leaving at six fifteen in the morning. Pastor Ford was picking me up at four thirty, which meant that if I went to sleep right now, I would only get five hours.

But it didn't matter, because I wouldn't even close my

eyes. How was I supposed to sleep when my whole life was about to change? Tomorrow, I would be in the city where my father lived.

Just thinking about that made me shiver, and I rolled out of the bed. At the window, I looked down in the alley filled with the same overflowing pails. With a sniff, I could smell the same ole garbage. There was no way my father would let us stay here when he saw this place. And my bedroom—he would take one look out this window and move me and Mama and D'Andre and 'em straight up out of Compton. Maybe we would all go back to New York with him.

Part of me was excited about living in New York. But the other side of me was crazy-sad. My sistahs and I were ride or die; when they rolled, I rolled, together always. And then, I was just getting to know Arjay. Did I want to leave California now?

Leaving was going to be really, really hard. But, truth—I would do anything to be with my daddy. And on the real, my sistahs would understand, 'cause they all had their fathers.

I jumped when the light came on in my room.

"You didn't hear me knocking?" my mother asked.

I shook my head.

"You have a lot on your mind," she said.

Mama had no idea. I wanted to tell her so bad, but I kept remembering what Mrs. Silver had said.

Mama sat down on my bed and patted the covers next to her. She said, "Come over here. Talk to me." She waited until I sat on the bed. "Are you excited?"

I nodded. "I can hardly stand it."

My mother smiled, but her eyes still didn't. "I know you're upset with me for not going with—"

I didn't even let her finish. "No, Mama. I understand."

She shook her head. "Girl, what did I tell you about lying?

You *don't* understand." The way she said it and the way she was smiling, I knew she wasn't mad. But then she got serious again. "You think I don't pay attention to you."

"It's okay, Mama. You work really hard."

She nodded. "But I want you to know, Vee, that I'm so proud of you. I'm proud of how you keep it together in school, I'm proud of what you're doing with the Divine Divas. You make me proud of the way you take care of your brothers. And the way you help around the house . . ." My mother looked straight into my eyes. "I'm proud to be your mother."

She was making me feel so good, and I wanted to pay her back—I wanted her to feel good, too. "Mama, I . . ."

When I stopped, she asked, "What is it?"

I tried to come up with the right way to say it. "I'm proud of you, too, Mama," was all that came out.

She hugged me. "I won't be in New York, but you know I'll be praying that you're safe and that the Divine Divas go all the way." Mama stood up and waited for me to lie back in the bed before she pulled the covers over me. Then she gave me a kiss and clicked off the light.

I turned over but didn't close my eyes. I wasn't even going to try to sleep.

♪ Chapter Thirty-one

We were just the four Divine Divas.

But we had our own entourage. There were the Three Ys Men and ten parents. And then there was Sybil and her husband and Turquoise. And of course Pastor Ford with her own mini-entourage—her daughter, her armor bearer, and Jackie, the minister of music.

That was twenty-four people from Hope Chapel on this plane. And there were going to be a lot more people from church coming to New York tomorrow.

I looked out the window; we were high above the clouds, floating east to New York. This was the first time in my life that I'd been on such a long plane ride.

I pulled my backpack from under my seat and took out the card that my mother had given to me this morning.

It still dark outside when Pastor Ford called and told us that she was downstairs. My mother walked down with me, carrying my suitcase.

Before I'd gotten inside the car, Mama had kissed me and

said, "I love you, Vee. I'm so proud of you." Then she'd pushed a card into my hand. "Don't open this until you get to New York."

When I'd gotten inside the car, I'd looked at the envelope. She had written the same words she'd just said: Don't Open Until New York!

Now I looked at those words again. How was I supposed to wait? I thought about it—I wasn't in New York, but I wasn't in L.A. either.

I tore the card open and almost choked when the money fell in my lap. I counted—ten twenty-dollar bills, two hundred dollars! I had never had that much money in my whole life.

It was hard not to cry as I read Mama's words:

I knew you would open this before you got to New York,
but I just wanted to tell you again that I'm proud of you.
Buy something special for yourself in New York. I love you!

Just as I wiped my tears away, Diamond looked at me. "What's wrong?"

I passed her the card with the money inside. "Wow!" She counted out the bills. Then she read what Mama wrote. "Well, look at the Queen of Mean. I knew she had some niceness in her."

I sniffed and smiled. "Yeah, she does." Diamond had really come up with the wrong name for my mother. She didn't understand our life. There was no way Diamond—or any of my sistahs—could ever know all that my mother went through every single solitary day. Mama wasn't mean, but she really was a queen.

"Hey," Diamond said in a low voice, "do you think your dad will come to the Apollo to see us?"

I hadn't thought about that. "Yeah, I'm sure he will."

Diamond smiled, and then she did what sistahs do; she held my hand.

All around, everyone was talking and laughing. In the row in front of us, Arjay and Troy were competing on their play-stations. And behind us, I was sure that Aaliyah was reading some book while India and Riley were talking.

I looked down at my card again. This was crazy-wild—I was on my way to New York, and now I had some money, too. Nothing but good stuff was happening to me.

♪ Chapter Thirty-two

There was a Hummer H2 outside—waiting for us!

"Now, don't get used to this," Pastor Ford said, even though all of us kids were cheering. "I got this for only the next three hours."

I was ahead of everyone and started rolling my suitcase toward our limo.

Sybil stopped me. "The luggage is going in another car," she said. "The Hummer only has room for the twenty-four people and no bags."

No problem for me. I dropped my bag right there, tossed my backpack over my shoulder, and was the first one to climb into the car.

It was crazy-cool inside. There were like three flat-screen TVs hanging from the ceiling and two bars—one on each side. I climbed to the front, near the driver, and was happy when Arjay plopped down next to me.

Diamond was behind him, and I thought she was going to

have a fit that he had taken her seat, but she was cool when she sat in between Arjay and Troy.

Everyone else piled inside behind us. When Pastor Ford got on last, she asked, "Is everybody on?"

There was a big "Yes," then Pastor hit a button on the console above her. "Okay, we're ready."

Now, that was tight! Pastor was talking to the driver through some kind of intercom. *Nothing but good stuff,* I thought.

The Hummer slowly moved away from the curb, and I twisted around so that I could see out the window real good. I wasn't about to miss one single solitary moment of New York.

The driver's voice came over a loudspeaker. "Okay," he said, "once we get out of the airport, we'll be heading down the Van Wyck Expressway to the Grand Central Parkway. We're gonna take the Triborough Bridge, and then we'll be in Harlem. I hear you guys want to see the Apollo Theater."

This time, I let everyone else say yes as I kept my eyes on the window. I couldn't stop looking at the houses and the cars. I mean, at any moment, we could be driving by my father's house. Or we could be riding next to my father's car.

"Why're you so serious?" Arjay asked.

I turned so that I could look right at him. When I'd first seen Arjay this morning, I'd been kind of surprised. Every day since we'd met, Arjay had always been wearing jeans. But today he was dressed up. In real nice black pants, a shirt, and even a tie, though I liked the way he wore it, so loose that it was almost hanging halfway down his shirt. Then I saw his parents and I knew what was up—his mother and father were dressed up, too, looking like they were going to church. I guess that was just the way the Lennox family rolled.

I answered, "I'm not serious. I just don't want to miss

anything." I turned back to the window. "I've never been to New York."

"Me neither, but we've got four days here. We've got lots of time to see lots of stuff, right?"

"True dat," I said, using one of his phrases.

He laughed, then got real close to me, like he was trying to get a better look out the window, too. When I inhaled, it was hard for me to think. He sure smelled good. I wondered what kind of cologne he was wearing, and then I wondered if my dad wore cologne, too.

We were moving kind of slow on this freeway. I glanced at my watch; it was only two o'clock in the afternoon, but traffic was just crawling along. Not that I minded. It helped me to see everything, though it didn't look like there was a whole lot to see. The houses all looked the same—really small and all gray, just different shades.

I wondered if my father lived in a house like this.

"So, this is the city, right?" I asked, not caring who answered.

"Yes," Diamond, the New York expert, said, "but technically, this is Queens. When people are talking about New York, they're only talking about Manhattan."

"That's not true," Aaliyah jumped in. "New York City has five boroughs, and Queens is one of them, just like Manhattan."

Diamond shot back, "But when people outside of New York talk about the city, they mean Manhattan."

I kinda shut out my sistahs. Diamond and Aaliyah were always fighting—that was their thing. It didn't matter to me if we were in the city or a borough or whatever. All I knew is that I was one step and one day closer to meeting my dad.

"We're coming up on the Triborough Bridge," the driver said over the speaker. "That's Manhattan to your left."

Everybody got quiet as we looked at the New York skyline.

I'd seen enough pictures to recognize the Empire State and Chrysler buildings. And I looked to the left, where I thought the World Trade Center used to be. I wondered what it had looked like before September 11. Even though I was only nine then, I remembered that day, and I wondered if my dad had been anywhere near the World Trade Center. That was just one of the things I couldn't wait to ask him.

"Okay," the driver said after we went over the bridge. "We're in Manhattan, on One hundred and twenty-fifth Street. Harlem, USA."

Harlem! I pressed my nose against the window, wanting to see this place I'd heard about my whole life.

I thought about my two hundred dollars. "Do they have good shopping in Harlem?" I asked, knowing for sure Diamond would be the one to answer me.

My best sistah said, "No, the best shopping is on Fifth Avenue." She turned to her mom. "Mother, I really want to go to the new Gucci Superstore. It's on Fifth," she said, like she was a New Yorker.

"We'll see, Diamond," Ms. Elizabeth answered.

Fifth Avenue shopping was definitely out for me. I bet Gucci didn't even sell a key chain that I could afford.

"Here's the Apollo," the driver said as he edged to the curb.

My sistahs were all saying, "Wow," but it looked like a regular ole theater to me. I knew it was a special place, because Sybil had told us about all the great Black singers who'd started out there. Maybe this would be the real beginning for us.

As we were looking out, people walking by slowed down and tried to peek into the Hummer. They must've thought some famous people were inside the big ole limousine.

That was funny! People thought we were famous.

"Can we get out?" Arjay asked.

"Not right now." Pastor Ford shook her head. "We'll have plenty of time here. I just wanted to give you guys a little tour, but we need to get to the hotel, check in, and rest up before dinner."

The Hummer moved back into traffic. After a couple of blocks, we turned and went down Frederick Douglass Boulevard.

"Hey, look," Troy yelled out. "There're Magic Johnson theaters here, too."

I kept staring out the window, looking at all the buildings: tall ones, brown ones, gray ones, brick ones. Did my father live or work in any of them?

In school, I'd learned that there were like ten million people in New York, and I think every single solitary one of them was out today.

"Oh, my God!" Diamond yelled and pointed out the window. "This is it!"

I looked at the sign—Fifth Avenue. Now I knew why my sistah was so caught up. I didn't know which side of the Hummer to look out of. We were passing all kinds of stores: FAO Schwarz, Louis Vuitton, Tiffany's.

"Mother, there's Gucci!"

There was store after store, but with my two hundred dollars, I wouldn't be able to step foot in any of them. Not that I cared. This kind of power-shopping was definitely my best sistah's thing.

"We just *have* to come back," Diamond said as if her life would end if she didn't. "Please, Daddy!"

"Now, how could I bring my girls all the way to New York and not do a little shopping?"

Diamond clapped her hands, and I grinned. Tomorrow at this time, I would have a dad who was just like Mr. Linden. Maybe my dad would take me shopping on Fifth.

Finally, the Hummer pulled in front of the Americana Hotel on Forty-ninth Street. There were so many of us inside that it took us like five minutes to all pile out of there. A Black man, dressed in the hotel's navy and gold uniform, held the door for us. Inside the lobby, we waited while the grown-ups went to the front desk.

It was a crazy-wow kind of building, with gold and mirrors and chandeliers everywhere. On the other side of the lobby, the guys were looking around like they were amazed, too.

"This is way, way better than the hotel we stayed in in San Francisco," India said.

"Of course it is," Diamond said, now a hotel expert. "The NYC is known for hotels. The most fabulous and most expensive hotels in the world are in New York City."

"That's not true," Aaliyah said. "There are fabulous hotels in Europe, too."

"But they're not as—"

They went at it again. I just let the two of them do their thing until Diamond's mother came over.

"I have your keys," she said. "You girls are sharing a suite."

Diamond clapped her hands, so I guessed that was a good thing.

Ms. Elizabeth said, "Diamond, you and Vee will share a bedroom." She handed us each a key, then turned to India and Aaliyah. "You girls will share the other bedroom. There's a living room in between where you can hang out together."

When everyone had their keys, Pastor Ford said to us, "Divas, the rules are the same." And then she turned to the guys and said, "No one leaves this hotel without an adult. Even when you're moving around in the hotel, travel together."

"All seven of us?" Troy asked, like that was the dumbest thing he'd ever heard.

Pastor Ford laughed. "That wouldn't be a bad idea. But, no. I just want you to walk around in groups of two—at least."

We all agreed and rolled our suitcases to the elevators. When the first one came, only the kids fit inside. We all went up together.

"What floor are you guys on?" Diamond asked.

"Eight." Arjay looked straight at me.

It felt like heat was rising underneath my skin. I had no idea why I was blushing.

"So are we!" Diamond said.

"Yeah, Riley and I are sharing a room," Troy said.

Still looking at me, Arjay said, "And I have my own room."

"Dang!" Diamond said. "It must be nice."

"Well, you know"—Arjay flicked his fingers against his shirt—"that's how I roll."

"Don't let him trick you," Troy laughed. "He's sharing a suite with his parents."

"Whatever, man." Arjay laughed, too. "I still got my own spot."

Why did Arjay keep looking at me? And why did it make me feel so funny?

When we got off the elevator and rolled our bags to our room, I had a new question—why did Arjay's room have to be right across from ours?

"Hey, you guys wanna catch dinner together?" Arjay asked.

"Yeah, that would be smooth," Diamond said.

"I thought Pastor said we were all going to dinner together," I said.

"We can get out of that," Troy said. "Let's order up a pizza and hang out in you guys' suite."

"That'll work," Diamond said, and India and Aaliyah agreed.

"Let's hook up in an hour," Arjay said, then asked me, "you have my number, right?"

Before I could tell him that I didn't, Diamond said, "I'll give it to her."

Arjay nodded, smiled at me, then went into his room.

We went into ours, and the moment I stepped inside the door, I stopped thinking about Arjay. All I could do was stare. Diamond and I were sharing the biggest bedroom I'd ever seen in my whole life. I'd never been anywhere near a castle, but I figured this was how one of the bedrooms in a castle would look. The walls were gold, and there were two big ole four-poster beds, two dressers, and two desks. And a huge flat-screen TV was hanging on the wall.

"Come here." Diamond grabbed my hand. "You've got to see this." She dragged me into the living room, where there was another flat-screen TV, two couches, lots of tables, a bar, and one wall that was just windows.

I ran into India and Aaliyah's bedroom, which was the same as ours. This whole place was crazy-stupid. It was one million times better than where I stayed.

"See, I told you," Diamond said to me. "The NYC is the best place in the whole wide world. I think when I become famous, I'm going to live here."

"You'd leave L.A.?" India asked.

Diamond thought about it for a moment. "Well, maybe I'll have a place in L.A. *and* New York. That's so cosmopolitan, you know. My girl Kimora Lee Simmons lives large like that."

India shook her head. "I can't imagine living anywhere besides L.A."

I didn't say a word. I wasn't ready to tell my sistahs that I might be leaving L.A.—and them.

"Okay, let's go change," Diamond demanded like she was in charge. "We have to get fierce for New York."

"Change? For what?" Aaliyah asked. "I thought we were just going to hang here."

"We still have to look good." Diamond rolled her eyes as if she couldn't believe she had to school us this way. "Listen to me. I'm the fashionista; I know what I'm talking about."

Diamond went into our bedroom, and India and Aaliyah went into theirs. But I stayed in the living room and looked out the gigantic window. I could see people below on Forty-ninth Street. And like I'd been doing ever since we got to New York, I wondered if any of those people were my father. Mrs. Silver had probably told him where I was staying. Maybe he couldn't wait to meet me and he'd come tonight.

"Vee!" Diamond yelled, like she was the boss of me.

Usually, she got on my nerves when she started acting like this. But I'd let her get away with it today, because after to-morrow, I didn't know what was going to happen. This might be the last weekend I'd ever spend with my sistahs.

♪Chapter Thirty-three

My hands and every part of my body were shaking as Diamond and I rode down the elevator. I hadn't wanted to make this call in the suite, because India or Aaliyah might have overheard me.

This was really about to happen.

Finally!

Since we'd gotten to New York, I'd had a hard time thinking about anything except for this morning. Even last night, when I should've had a great time, all I'd been able to think about was my father.

As we'd sat in the suite and eaten the four pizzas that Pastor had ordered for us, everyone had been laughing and talking—except for me. Even though Arjay had sat next to me the whole time, I still hadn't been able to have a good time. All I'd been able to do was keep counting down the hours until I was going to see my father.

Then, when I'd gone to bed, I hadn't slept. I hadn't been able to wait for the sun to shine, and when light had begun to come through our window, I had jumped out of bed. I hadn't really had anything to do, so I'd just read through all the chats I'd had with Mrs. Silver, just waiting for more hours to pass.

Now, it was time.

I looked over at Diamond; she looked like she was shaking as much as I was. "Are you scared?" she asked when the elevator doors opened.

I shook my head as we walked into the lobby. "No," I said, although in a way I was.

We found a chair far away from the front desk, surrounded by a bunch of big ole plants so that no one would see us. Diamond handed me her cell.

I stared at it for a moment before I dialed the number that Mrs. Silver had given me. Diamond leaned over, and I held the phone so that she could hear, too.

The lady answered on the first ring. "Hello."

I frowned. Her voice sounded really strange. Like she was a robot or something.

"Why does she sound so weird?" Diamond whispered.

I put my finger over her lips, telling her to be quiet. I didn't know why Mrs. Silver sounded like that—maybe that's just the way old ladies talked.

"Are you in New York?" Mrs. Silver asked.

"Yes, can I talk to my father?"

"Not yet. First, I have to be paid."

Paid. My heart began to beat fast. Mrs. Silver had told me she didn't have any fees. "I didn't know this was going to cost anything," I said. "I only have two hundred dollars."

"Don't tell her that!" Diamond hissed. "She'll take all your money."

I didn't care. I'd give Mrs. Silver every single one of my two hundred dollars so that I could see my dad.

Mrs. Silver said, "I had some extra expenses finding your father, but don't worry. Your father will pay the money."

I started shaking again. My father wanted to meet me so bad, he would pay! "So, if he's going to give you the money, why doesn't he want to talk to me?" I asked. I knew that I was probably going to see him in an hour or something like that, but I couldn't wait.

"He doesn't want to give me any money until he's sure it's you. He wants to see you in person."

That made sense. "What time are you guys going to get here?"

"You haven't told anyone, have you?" she asked, not answering my question.

"No."

"Good, then you need to come and meet us. We'll be at the Shaggy Dog Diner in Times Square. Any cab driver will know where that's at."

"No!" Diamond shouted, and I pushed her away.

"What was that?" Mrs. Silver asked.

"Nothing, I'm in the lobby of the hotel and someone just walked by." I made a warning face at Diamond; she nodded and sat back down next to me.

I said, "I thought you and my dad were coming here."

"No, you have to meet us."

"But I can't. I'm not allowed to leave the hotel without an adult."

"My car broke down and I don't have the money to take a cab. I'm an older woman. I can't spend money that way."

"Get the money from my dad."

"I told you," she said, sounding like she was starting to get angry. "Your father wants to be sure you're his daughter first. Just meet us."

I took a deep breath. There was no way I could go somewhere

in a city I didn't know to meet someone I'd never seen before.

"Look," Mrs. Silver said, "if you don't want to meet your father—"

"No!" This time, I was the one who shouted. "I'll be there."

"Meet us in an hour. At exactly eleven fifteen. Remember, you have to come alone, because that's how your father wants it. If he sees you with anyone else, he'll just leave."

"Okay," I said, not really feelin' meeting them by myself. But this was my only chance.

"Don't worry," Mrs. Silver said, as if she could tell that I was a little scared. "You'll be safe with me; that's why we're meeting in the daytime. And I've checked this man out. You're safe."

"Okay," I said, this time a little stronger.

Mrs. Silver said, "I can protect you. But you have to come alone," she warned again.

"Okay."

Diamond jumped up, acting like she didn't care if Mrs. Silver heard her or not.

I ignored my girl, wrote down the address, and told Mrs. Silver that I would meet her and my dad in an hour.

"No!" Diamond snatched her phone away from me when I hung up. "You *cannot* leave. You know the rules."

"I have to go."

"I don't have a good feeling about this."

I bit the corner of my lip. Neither did I, but what could I do? "I have to go, Diamond. I can't get this close. I have to meet my father."

"Okay," Diamond said as she stuck out her chest, "then I'm going with you."

Now I was the one shaking my head like I was crazy. "No

way. You heard her. If my dad sees me with anyone, he'll walk away."

"That doesn't make sense."

"It doesn't have to make sense to you. Only to me. You have your dad." I was almost crying. "I have to go!"

Arjay jumped out from behind the sofa. "Hey, y'all." He grinned. "Where're you going?"

I couldn't believe he'd been hiding like that. Had he heard anything?

He repeated his question, and now he wasn't grinning anymore. "Where're you going?"

"None of your business!" I was like crazy-mad. Why was everyone trying to get in my way? This was the most important thing that was ever going to happen to me, and everybody was messing it up.

Arjay's eyes got real small. "What're you guys up to?" He looked back and forth between me and Diamond.

"I said, none of your business!" Then I glared at Diamond. With my eyes, I warned her that she better not say a word.

As I rushed to the elevator, I knew Diamond wasn't going to give me up. She might not like what I was doing, but we were sistahs. We always had each other's back. If I couldn't count on anything else, I could count on that. Trust and know.

Inside the suite, I grabbed my backpack and checked my wallet to make sure I had all my money just in case I had to pay Mrs. Silver for something. When I rushed into the hallway, I bumped right into India.

"Hey," she said. "Where're you going?"

Before I could think, I said, "For a walk."

"On the track in the gym? I'll go with you."

"No!"

India frowned. "What's wrong with you?"

"Nothing. I'm not going to the gym. I'm going for a walk around the block."

"We're not supposed to leave the hotel by ourselves."

"I won't be by myself. Diamond's waiting for me downstairs," I lied.

"We're not supposed to leave the hotel without an adult."

"Dang! Who are you, the police? Just leave me alone!" I didn't even wait for the elevator. I went to the staircase and started running down the steps.

I knew I had hurt India's feelings, just like I'd probably hurt Arjay. And Diamond. But when I came back in a couple of hours with my father, they would all be so excited that they would forgive me.

In the lobby, I peeked to see if Diamond and Arjay were hanging around. But even though the lobby was filled with people, there was no one from Hope Chapel.

I walked real fast, not stopping until I got outside.

"Can I help you, miss?"

I hoped the doorman wasn't spying for Pastor Ford.

"I . . . I want to take a cab to this place." I showed him the piece of paper.

He frowned a little. "That's in Times Square." Then he looked at me. "You're going there by yourself?"

I tried to act like I was strong and brave and old enough to do this. "Yes," I nodded. "I'm going to meet my father."

"Oh, then, that's okay." The man raised his hand, and a yellow car rolled up right in front of us. While I climbed inside, he told the driver where I was going.

As we pulled away from the hotel, I looked out the back

216

window. The next time I saw that building, the next time I saw Diamond, or any of my sistahs, I would be with my father.

I put in my earplugs and turned up the volume on my favorite song.

Now I didn't feel so scared.

Chapter Thirty-four

When the taxi stopped in front of the Shaggy Dog Diner, I was almost too scared to get out.

Not sure what I was supposed to do, I sucked it up and said to the driver, "How much money do I have to give you?"

The man pointed to the meter, and showed me the numbers 4.65. I gave him a five-dollar bill and said, "Keep the change," the way I'd seen people do on TV.

I got out of the cab and peeped at the big sign for *The Color Purple* on the theater across the street. As I stood there, everybody kept bumping me, rushing by, almost knocking me over. Even though it was daytime, there were so many lights. And so much noise.

I tried to stare into the face of every man who passed by. But they were moving too fast. Then I remembered. My father was in the diner.

Taking a deep breath, I stepped into the Shaggy Dog. It was kind of a dark spot, and it took a couple of seconds for my eyes to get used to it. There weren't many people inside—just three men all sitting at different tables. And none of them looked up. I wasn't sure what I was supposed to do, so I just slipped into one of the booths.

I stared again at the three men—one White, two Black— but one just kept drinking coffee, one was reading his newspaper, and the third one was staring out the window. Didn't look like any of them were waiting to meet their daughter. I turned to the window; maybe I'd see Mrs. Silver and my dad before they walked in.

"You're not doing any business here, are you?"

I looked up and frowned at the waitress. "Business?"

"Yeah."

I shook my head.

"Okay, do you want to order?"

I shook my head again. I didn't want to open my wallet in front of anyone, not with all the money I had. And anyway, my stomach was dippin' and flippin'; I didn't want to eat anything. "Is it okay if I sit here? I'm waiting for my father."

"Your father?" The woman chuckled. "Yeah, you can wait here. But no business, okay?"

When she walked away, I shrugged. I had no idea what she was talking about, but as long as she let me wait, I was cool.

I sat. I waited. I looked at my watch. The first man got up and walked out. More minutes passed. Then another one left. Fifteen minutes went by, and soon I was the only customer left in the diner.

I wanted to listen to my song, but I was afraid that I would miss Mrs. Silver and my dad calling me when they came in.

More time passed, and no one even walked inside. Every minute that went by made me sadder and sadder. Made me think that Mrs. Silver wasn't going to come. Made me think that I wasn't going to meet my dad today. Made me think that this had all been a stupid trick. All of that thinking made me want to cry.

"Veronique?"

Just when I'd lost all hope! I lifted my head and stared into the face of a man. But he was a White man. I knew *he* wasn't my father. And he looked really scary—with little eyes and a big nose. And his lips were covered by all of the hair on his face.

I frowned. "Who are you?"

"Mrs. Silver's son. My mother asked me to take you to your father." He stopped talking and looked around the restaurant. His eyes blinked fast.

"Where's my father?"

"I'll take you to him."

I shook my head. I wasn't that stupid. "Just tell me, where's my father?"

"Do you want to see him?"

What do you think? I said, "Yes!" There was a small part of me that was still hoping all of this was for real.

"Then come with me. Your father is right outside."

My hope was back. I peeked out the window, but all I saw were like dozens of people walking fast down the street. Nobody stopped to look at us.

"Come on, you have to move quickly," the man whispered. "Or your dad will go away. He doesn't want anyone to see him."

"Why not?"

"Come on." He grabbed my arm. "Your dad is right around the corner."

I really wanted that to be the truth, but it didn't feel like the truth anymore.

"Come on," the man said, pulling me up.

I stood face-to-face, toe-to-toe.

And I was mad.

Looking into his face, I had all kinds of bad feelings.

"You have to come with me," he said.

I wasn't that big a fool. "No!"

The man said, "Would you be quiet!"

"Who are you?" I asked, still trying to wiggle away from him. He didn't need to have his hands on me like that.

"I already told you. Do you want to see your father or not?"

What kind of stupid question was that? Of course, I did. That was why I'd spent all these weeks talking to Mrs. Silver. That was why I was sitting in this dark, smelly place talking to this scary man.

"Come on," he repeated, trying to pull me.

"I'm not going anywhere," I shouted, hoping that the waitress would come over and ask what was going on.

"Hey," she finally called out.

Thank God! I thought. But she just yelled at us from the counter, "I told you, no business in here. Take that mess outside."

What?

He yelled back, "We're leaving." And then to me, he said, "Come on," as he squeezed my arm.

I tried to yank away from him, but his fingers were gripping me so tight that it felt like the blood had stopped flowing through my arms. "Stop it!" I screamed. I looked around, praying that someone would walk through that door.

Just when I had that thought, I heard, "Veronique!"

The man and I both froze still.

"Arjay!"

I had never in my whole life been so happy to see anyone.

Then time moved like a slow-motion movie. The man pushed me against the table.

"Ouch!" I screamed, feeling like my back was broken.

The man moved toward the back door, and Arjay ran after him, knocking down a couple of chairs. I lay on the floor for a minute, until Arjay came back to help me.

He pulled me up and hugged me. He held me so tight, it was hard to breathe. But I didn't care; I wanted to stay right there with his arms around me.

"Are you all right?"

I nodded, because I was afraid that if I said anything, I would cry. Then I would look like a fool *and* a big ole baby.

"What were you thinking?" he asked me.

What was I supposed to say? Arjay could never understand. He had his father—just like my sistahs.

"Take that mess out of here!" the waitress yelled as she picked up the chair the man had knocked over when he'd run through the door. "I told you, no business."

She was still grumbling when Arjay took my hand and led me toward the door. I didn't say a word—just walked out behind him, from the dark diner into the light.

People bumped past us as Arjay raised his hand. A taxi stopped right away. He told the driver the name of our hotel before he flipped open his cell phone.

"Yo, Diamond; I got her. Tell everybody she's all right."

The car rolled through Times Square, past all the buildings with neon lights, and the bigger-than-life billboards of men in underwear and women holding perfume bottles. That was when the first tears came to my eyes. But I wiped them away. I wasn't going to do that; not in front of Arjay.

But I was still shaking. It wasn't until Arjay took my hand that I calmed down. And I felt safe.

Safe, but still stupid. A big ole stupid fool. Mrs. Silver had seemed so real. And meeting my father—that had seemed real, too.

But it had all been a fairy tale that was never, ever going to happen.

♪ Chapter Thirty-five

Arjay squeezed my hand before he pulled me out of the taxi. And it was a good thing he was holding onto me, because when we walked into the lobby, Diamond almost tackled me to the floor.

"Are you okay?" She hugged me tight.

"Yeah," I whispered. "And thanks for giving me up. Thanks for sending Arjay. He saved me."

But I didn't get the chance to say anything else. It seemed like everyone from Hope Chapel had packed the lobby and surrounded me.

Mr. Heber, Aaliyah's father, was all in my face. "Who met you at the diner, Veronique?"

I glanced at Diamond; she looked down at her feet, and I figured she'd given me up to more than just Arjay. But how could I be mad about it?

"Veronique, tell me everything," Mr. Heber said.

I really didn't want to talk about this. Just wanted to go up to my room, get in the bed, and pull the covers over my head.

I said, "I was supposed to meet the lady I was talking to on the computer, but . . ." I stopped right there.

The way Mr. Heber looked at Pastor Ford, I knew I didn't have to say anything else.

"Veronique and Arjay"—Pastor Ford pointed at us—"come with me and Heber up to my suite. We need to talk." She waved everyone else away. "We'll all meet down here at two like we planned, since we don't have to be at the Apollo for rehearsal until six."

Before I could take one step, Ms. Elizabeth said, "Do you know how worried we were?" She hugged me.

India and Aaliyah were right behind her. India's eyes were red, swollen, and sad.

"I'm sorry," I said before India could say anything.

"I was so scared," India said, "when Diamond told us where you went. I knew I should've gone with you no matter what you said."

Even Troy and his parents gave me a hug.

"Girl, you better not do anything like that again. Know what I'm sayin'?" Troy gave me a soft punch on my arm.

The only people who didn't say a word to me were Arjay's parents. They were standing against the wall, whispering to Arjay. His dad's hands were flying through the air as he talked, and every couple of seconds, his mother would look at me and then turn away like she couldn't stand to look at me. What was up with that?

Pastor Ford waved Arjay over. Then she put her arms around me and led me to the elevator.

"Can I go with you guys?" Diamond asked. "I know every-thing and can fill in anything Vee doesn't remember."

Pastor nodded, and Diamond took my hand. My sistah had given that big ole explanation, but I knew what was up. Diamond just had my back—like she always did.

Nobody said a word until we got to the suite. Pastor and Mr. Heber stared at me as if they wanted me to start talking.

So, I did. "All I wanted to do was find my father." That was enough, I figured.

"How were you going to do that?" Pastor Ford asked.

Now see, that was a dirty trick. Downstairs, Pastor had seemed like she'd been happy to see me. But now, she sat with her arms crisscrossed and her lips pressed together like she was crazy-mad.

I just hoped that she would still love me. The thought that she might not made my lips tremble.

Diamond must've seen what was happening, because she started talking. "We were looking for her dad online and then we met this lady, Mrs. Silver, who helped children find their parents, especially missing fathers." Diamond kept talking, but Pastor and Mr. Heber kept looking at me.

My sistah filled them in on everything—from the Child Services Agency and all the pictures we sent to her, to the phone call this morning.

"And this Mrs. Silver arranged to meet you?" Pastor asked.

I nodded. "Only she didn't show up," I said, keeping my eyes away from Arjay. I knew that right about now, he thought that I was totally stupid.

Mr. Heber said, "What happened at the diner?"

I took a deep breath, because Diamond couldn't help me with this. I told them about Mrs. Silver's son and how he tried to take me away. "That's when Arjay got there," I finished.

Saying all of that out loud made me know just how crazy I'd been to believe all of that.

"What did the man look like?" Mr. Heber asked.

I remembered every bit of his scary face and described him.

He asked, "Do you remember anything else, Arjay?"

"Nah, that's pretty much it. I didn't really get a good look at him. As soon as he heard me call Vee's name, he cut out of there. I didn't go after him 'cause when I looked back, Vee was on the ground. I had to make sure she was okay."

"Good thing you didn't," Mr. Heber said. "You don't know if he was armed or what."

Armed? Oh, my God! This was some crazy-mess that I'd gotten everyone into. I'd never thought about Mrs. Silver—or that man—having a gun or something.

"You kids got off easy." Mr. Heber was shaking his head.

"Definitely," Pastor added, making me feel like two cents. "Neither of you were supposed to leave this hotel."

Could this get any worse? I mean, wasn't it enough that I was in trouble? Did Arjay have to be knee-deep in it, too?

"In fact, all three of you were wrong." Pastor turned to Diamond. "Once Veronique left, you two should have come to us."

I couldn't take it. "Pastor," I said before she beat them up any more. "It was all my fault. They were just trying to help me."

"It doesn't matter. You all broke the rules, period!"

I wanted to crawl right into the ground. It was bad enough being yelled at, but Diamond and Arjay were in trouble for all the dumb things I'd done.

"Pastor, I need to take Veronique and Arjay to the police station and report this. I have some friends here in New York, and we need to file a report—"

"No!" I was shaking my head. "He didn't do anything to me. There's nothing to tell the police, because I got away."

"And you were very blessed," Mr. Heber said, "because you don't know where this man might have taken you or what he would have done to you!"

I closed my eyes.

"Ah Heber," Pastor said, "I think Veronique knows—"

Aaliyah's father held up his hand. "Pastor, she needs to hear this. Diamond needs to hear this, too. In fact, I need to get India and Aaliyah. You don't know what that man would have done to you, Veronique. And the next girl may not be as blessed as you were today. That's why we need to report this. We need to give the police a chance to get him off the internet and off the streets."

I still wasn't sure.

"Veronique," he said, with a much softer voice this time, "you could be saving someone's life." He took my hand, and I looked down at how his large fingers almost covered my whole hand. Like he was protecting me. The way my father was supposed to.

I looked up and said, "Okay."

"Good," he said. "But first, I want to log onto your personal page account. See if we can capture some of those messages and chats."

"I have those," I said, reaching into my bag. "I kept most of our chats."

"What were you trying to be, a little detective?" Mr. Heber asked as he glanced through the papers. He smiled a little, like he was trying to make me feel better.

"No, I just wanted to keep them because," I lowered my eyes and my voice, "it made me feel closer to my father."

Pastor came over to where I was sitting. "Can you guys leave us alone for a little while?"

Mr. Heber looked at his watch.

"We have plenty of time," Pastor said. "Let's meet in the lobby in an hour; we'll go to the station and still be back in plenty of time to make it over to the Apollo."

Mr. Heber nodded and patted my shoulder. Diamond squeezed my hand, and Arjay hugged me.

The whole time they were walking away, I wanted to scream, *"Come back."* I always loved my time alone with Pastor, but I knew this wasn't going to be one of those feel-good times.

It was my third cup of water and Pastor just sat on the couch looking at me. I was getting full, and I guess it didn't make much sense to keep drinking. Stalling wasn't going to stop nothin'.

I put the glass down. "I'm sorry, Pastor."

She nodded. "I know you are. But that doesn't stop me from being disappointed. I told you girls to come to me if you were going through anything. But instead . . ." She closed her eyes and shook her head like she was tired. "Did you hear what Heber said? The man could have had a gun. What were you thinking?"

If she was trying to scare me, she was doing a great job. "Pastor, I'm so sorry," I said, over and over.

She looked at me and didn't say anything.

"I was just . . . I just wanted . . ." And then I couldn't hold it back anymore. Tears gushed out of me like a faucet. "Pastor, all I wanted to do was find my father."

"Why didn't you ever tell me?"

I shrugged and sniffed. "I thought I could do it myself."

"But I would have helped you."

"I know." I nodded. "But then, suppose you helped and then we found out that my dad . . . didn't want me." I said the words that I'd been thinking, and it really hurt. "That's probably why he's not with me now."

"Oh, Veronique." She pulled me close to her.

I stayed right there and cried until I didn't have any more tears left.

Without letting go, Pastor said, "You know, I spent a good part of my life without my father."

I looked up at her.

She said, "My mom passed away when I was young, and my father wasn't around all that much after that. My brothers and sisters and I were moved from one relative to the next. It took me a lot of years to get over that. So, I know exactly how you feel."

I wasn't sure if she really did. "It's so hard, especially when I look at Diamond, India, and Aaliyah and they're with their dads."

"It's a horrible feeling, I know."

"So what did you do to feel better?"

"I turned to God."

Of course that's what Pastor would say, but how was I supposed to do that? I was just a kid—God didn't listen to me the way he listened to her.

She said, "And you can do that same thing."

"I pray to God all the time. But it's not the same as having a real father."

"You're right, it's not the same. It's better."

I didn't have a single, solitary clue why Pastor would say something crazy like that. I mean, God was in heaven. How could that be as good as having a father that I could see and hug and kiss right here on earth?

"You know, Veronique," Pastor Ford continued, "when we say that God is our father, that's not just some nice cliché. It's the real deal. God is alive, and He can help you through everything that an earthly father can."

At first, I was just going to keep my thoughts to myself, but Pastor always said that we could talk to her about anything. So I figured I might as well tell her what I was thinking. "God can't do everything," I said. "Not the way a real father can.

Not the way my sistah's fathers do things with them. Like in sixth grade, their fathers took them to the father-daughter dance, and I couldn't go."

Pastor Ford held me tighter when I said that. "I didn't know about that."

"This is gonna sound stupid, Pastor, but I've never even bought a Father's Day card for anyone."

She waited for a little while before she said, "That doesn't sound stupid at all." She squeezed me even tighter. "But God knew it was going to be like this. This isn't a surprise to Him. It would be wonderful to have your father with you, and who knows, one day, you may." With the tips of her fingers, she lifted my chin and made me look at her. "But the truth is that since God gave you *this* life, He will always take care of you. Before you were born, he knew your past, your present, and your future. He wants you to be your best, so He'll make sure that the people who are supposed to be in your life are there."

"But why did He do it this way, Pastor? It doesn't make sense that He gave some people fathers and He didn't give me one."

"You have a father, Veronique. Don't you ever think that you don't. You just don't happen to know him."

"It feels like the same thing to me—not having one and not knowing him."

Pastor Ford gave me a small smile. "You're such a wise, wise girl. But you have to realize that you're not supposed to understand everything about God. I don't know why God wanted you to live your life this way, but let me tell you what I do know. I know God has a purpose for you, something He wants *you* to do with *your* life. I know that He'll give you everything you need to accomplish that purpose. Now, maybe God knew that Diamond and the other girls needed their fathers to follow through on His plans for their lives. Maybe God knew that you needed something else. Maybe He knew that you needed your mother more. Like maybe He knew that Aaliyah needed her father more."

It was almost like Pastor was saying that not knowing my father was a good thing.

"Don't get it twisted; I'm not saying that God wouldn't like it better if your father was here. He created families to be together. It was sin that came into the world that changed God's plans," Pastor said. "But He's still in control; He still knows everything.

"You have to stop trying to figure out *why* your life is the way it is and focus on *what* you're supposed to do." She took my hands inside of hers. "God has great plans for you. Just look at the gifts He's given you—your music, your political savvy, your intelligence. Your mother, your brothers, your friends. He even gave you me." She smiled. "You have so much. Focus on the blessings, not the burdens."

After what happened to me today, I didn't think I would ever smile again. But that's exactly what I did when I hugged my pastor as tight as I could.

Focus on the blessings—that was a good tip, 'cause I had lots of them.

"Okay, young lady," Pastor said, pulling me up. "We have to take care of some business."

I nodded. Even though I still felt like there was a big ole hole in my heart, Pastor Ford had really helped me feel better. It was still hard to believe that my dream was over, but I guess I just had to find a new dream.

One that didn't have anything to do with my dad.

♪ Chapter Thirty-six

As Diamond would say, these black patent-leather boots were fierce. I was glad that I'd let Diamond talk me into them, because they looked crazy-cool with this silver metallic minidress. The good thing was I didn't have to worry about slipping and sliding across the stage, because I'd gotten a good workout in these last night during rehearsal. And even this morning in our suite we were practicing.

I looked in the mirror one more time. Even though my sistahs were around me laughing and talking and all excited, it was hard for me to feel good. All I really wanted to do was lay down and cry every time I thought about my dad. Really, there was nothing to think about, since it had been all made up. Mrs. Silver didn't even exist—at least that's what the police had told me when Pastor Ford, Mr. Heber, Arjay, and I had gone to the station. When I'd told them about how weird Mrs. Silver had sounded on the phone, the policeman had told me that was probably a mechanical voice used to make a man sound like a woman.

"Lord, have mercy!" Pastor Ford had said when the police had told us that.

Truth—that was some crazy-weird stuff. I knew I had to be careful on the internet talking to a man, but I'd thought I'd been safe and smart because I'd been chatting with a woman.

I'd been fooled big-time, and the policeman had told me so.

"You have to be careful, young lady," he'd said to me. "Anybody can tell you anything on the internet. Never arrange to meet with someone you don't know. That's always an invitation for trouble."

I could still hear the policeman's voice in my head.

But I needed to shake it off and suck it up. All I needed to be thinking about was getting on that stage and bringing it, because if we didn't win, it would be my fault.

When I felt the hand on my shoulder, I almost jumped right out of my skin.

"You're a little bit nervous, huh?" Pastor Ford asked.

Even though I was standing in front of the mirror, I hadn't even seen her behind me.

"Come over here." She took my hand and led me into the corner, away from my sistahs, who were primping and posing, checking on their outfits. "We need to pray."

I thought we were all going to pray together, but you never said no to Pastor when she wanted to talk to God. I closed my eyes and waited for Pastor to do her thing.

But after a couple of seconds, it was still quiet. I opened one eye and peeked at her. Pastor Ford had her head bowed, but her lips weren't moving.

Then it hit me—she was waiting for me to pray! Now, I knew how to pray a good word, but how was I supposed to do this in front of Pastor Ford? I mean, there was no one who could send up a prayer like she could. It was crazy-ridiculous that she wanted *me* to do this.

She said, "Go ahead."

I took a deep breath. "Dear God," I began, "thank You for letting us be in New York for this competition. Thank You for letting us get this far, and bless us tonight as we sing—"

"Veronique," Pastor whispered my name.

I looked up, and she was staring at me. "Talk to God from your heart. Don't say what you think I want to hear. Talk to Him about what's right there." She pressed her finger against my chest, then closed her eyes again.

I started praying, "God, thank You for keeping me safe in New York. I know You're probably as upset with me as Pastor is, but all I wanted to do was to find my father. I don't know why You didn't let me find him, but You still kept me safe. Even though I was scared the whole time, I knew You were with me. And forgive me for lying and not telling anybody; I just wanted to meet my dad so bad. But even though I still want to meet him, I'm going to focus on the blessings and not the burdens. I'm going to concentrate on what You want me to do. And then, maybe You'll let me find him. Thank You." I was glad that I was finished. And then I added, "Oh, and Amen, too."

Pastor Ford hugged me, then said, "Now you go out on that stage with your *sistahs* and rock it!"

I cracked up. Listen to Pastor, being all hip. I guess Pastor Ford was what Sybil always wanted us to be . . . she was hip and holy for real!

The stage was dark.

"Ladies and gentlemen," I heard Kirk Franklin announce.

He was the celebrity guest for this round of the competition. "Give it up for the Divine Divas!"

The applause started as the curtain slowly rolled up. Then the track began.

"Everybody!" We sang the first note and held it. The crowd cheered.

"Come on, y'all," we sang. We started clapping and strutted right to the edge of the stage.

"Everybody get up!"

Then the guys came out, and the crowd went crazy-wild. Troy backed up against me, and then he snaked around to Aaliyah.

We kept dancin' and dippin', struttin' and kickin'.

"Send the praises up!"

We twisted around; our backs were now to the crowd as the guys did their dance, weaving through us.

"And the blessings will flow." I sang my part while Arjay wiggled in front of me.

We sang and danced, and even though I couldn't see anyone from the stage, I could hear the crowd rocking with us.

When we got to the last chorus, the guys came out front and did that break-dance thing.

"Get on up and dance!" We sang that last verse in perfect harmony and held our pose for five seconds.

But the crowd was already clapping and stomping and screaming. It even looked like some people were trying to rush the stage.

We started clapping, then ran off, all out of breath.

"Man, I can't believe we did that!" Arjay said to Troy and Riley as they hugged and bumped knuckles.

Troy said, "Yeah, that was stupid!"

"Ridiculous," Riley added.

My sistahs and I were hugging each other before the guys

hugged us, too. When Arjay hugged me, he kissed me on my cheek. And every bad feeling I'd been having since yesterday went away.

Sybil met us behind the curtains. "The crowd—they're still clapping for you guys!" she yelled.

I knew we had nailed it; I'd felt it when we'd been on the stage. But even though I was grinning and laughing, after everything we'd been through with the other contests, I wasn't about to start thinking that we'd won.

The crowd started shouting, "Divine Divas! Divine Divas! Divine Divas!"

"Should we go back out there?" Diamond asked, already moving toward the stage.

"No," Sybil said. "Remember the rules, one bow only."

"So, what do we do now?" Riley asked.

"Just wait until they call y'all back on the stage," Sybil told him. "It'll be just a couple of minutes, since you guys were last."

Just as she said that, the nine other groups came out from the back. Some of the girls came over and congratulated us. But they didn't spend too much time talking to me or my sistahs. They were all over the guys.

Dang! We were the ones who had done all the singing. But I really couldn't hate. Truth—the guys were all that. But one thing I didn't like was the way a couple of those girls were hanging all over Arjay.

"Ladies and gentlemen, let's welcome all the groups back onto the stage."

We were closest, so we started moving first. But when I looked back, Arjay was the only one not following us. He was still grinning in those girls' faces.

"Arjay!" I shouted, like I was the boss of him.

He looked up. "Sorry," he said when he caught up to me.

He put his hand on my back, and right away I didn't feel so bad anymore.

On the stage, Arjay and I stood next to each other as Roberto Hamilton, the president of the Glory 2 God label, talked.

"We're taking four groups down to Miami for the finals," Mr. Roberto said. "And that's going to be a special time, because some major stars have agreed to mentor our groups."

We all clapped to that. Man, I wondered who would be working with us!

As Mr. Roberto kept talking about what was going to happen in Miami, Arjay leaned over to me. "You know you're wearing that dress, right?" he whispered.

I didn't look at him, but I'm sure he could see me grinning. I felt that heat rising underneath my skin again. Arjay just did that to me.

Mr. Roberto said, "Now, here's the moment you've all been waiting for. The first group going to Miami is . . ."

Arjay took my hand and squeezed it. I closed my eyes and tried not to think of the bad things that had happened to me in New York. Just wanted to think about this moment.

"The Divine Divas!"

It took a moment for his words to go from my ears to my brain. Arjay picked me up and swung me around.

We were going to the finals!

We cheered, hugged each other, then ran to the front of the stage.

It was hard to just stand there as Mr. Roberto announced the other three groups.

Finally, the end of the announcements came. "Ladies and gentlemen, please congratulate all of the groups going to Miami and all of the young men and women who made it to New York!"

As we all congratulated each other, the audience kept applauding. And then the stage started filling up with the folks from Hope Chapel.

"I am so proud of you," Pastor Ford said as she hugged me.

I looked around, and everyone else was with their parents. But I didn't feel as bad as I usually did. I was remembering the blessings.

Pastor Ford backed up a little when her cell phone rang. "I think this is for you," she said.

Her cell rang and it was for me? I took the phone from my pastor.

"Hey, baby. Congratulations!"

"Hi, Mama!" I don't think I'd ever been so glad to speak to my mother.

"So, you're going to Miami, huh?"

"Yeah, how did you know?"

"You must've forgotten who I am. I'm your mama. I know everything."

We laughed together.

"Can you believe it!" I said.

"I heard you guys smoked it."

I cracked up. Guess Pastor Ford wasn't the only hip grown-up around.

"Vee, I'm so proud of you."

"Thanks, Mama."

"And, Vee . . ."

"Yes."

"When you get home, there are some things we have to talk about."

Uh-oh. I'd been hoping that Pastor wouldn't give me up but I guess she'd had to. Just like my sistahs had my back, the grown-ups had to do the same thing. I just hoped my mom wasn't going to be crazy-mad and do something like ground me for a year.

Mama said, "We have a lot to talk about—what went on in New York and . . . who's going to stay with your brothers while you and I are hanging in Miami."

My mouth opened wide. "You're gonna go with me?" I asked, not sure that I was hearing right.

"Of course. I'm not going to let my daughter become a star without me. I'm gonna be right there yelling and cheering for my baby."

Oh, my God. I could just see it now—my mother acting silly in the audience. And truth—that was gonna be crazy-cool with me.

"I love you, Mama," I said before I clicked off the phone. Then I wrapped my arms around Pastor Ford's neck. "Thank you."

Pastor Ford leaned back. "Oh, please. You can use my cell anytime."

"Not for that," I said. "For helping me to remember my blessings, 'cause I sure got a lot of them."

Pastor Ford kissed my cheek. "Yes, you do." She looked around the room. "You're all blessed."

I looked at my girls and then at Troy, Riley, and Arjay, who, I guess, were my boys now. My boys! How cool was that?

I had sistahs, and now I had more brothers.

The Divine Divas.

The Three Ys Men.

We were on our way to the finals, and we were blessed— big-time. Trust and know.

Readers Group Guide

Summary

Best friends Diamond, India, Veronique, and Aaliyah are high school sophomores who have been friends since childhood. After forming a singing group—The Divine Divas—in order to enter a gospel talent search and winning several levels of competition, the girls must prepare for the semifinals in New York City. This third installment in the Divas' story is told by Veronique, also known as Vee, who dreams of finding her father and rescuing her family from their "ghetto-normal" life. Of the four Divas, Vee is the only one for whom money is scarce. She lives with her mother (who works two jobs) and her four younger brothers in an apartment in Compton. She often wonders why the Divas like her at all. But her sistahs have always stood by her, and she's about to test their loyalty: Vee has a plan to find her father and meet him when they go to New York City, certain that once he sees her he will want her (and her mother and brothers) to move in with him so they can be a family. She secretly sets up a MySpace page and is soon receiving messages from a woman who promises that she can help. But when Vee arrives at their planned meeting, she's surprised to find a man waiting for her—and he isn't her father.

Discussion Points

1. Even though she doesn't even remember him, Veronique misses her father desperately. What does he represent to her? What do you think she's really yearning for when she dreams of finding him?

2. Veronique frequently feels that the Divas wouldn't hang out with her if they knew what her life was really like. Compare and contrast Vee's "ghetto-normal" life with the lives of the other Divas. Do you think her feelings are based on reality or are they self-imposed? Give examples from the novel to support your opinion.

3. If you've read the previous two novels in this series, how do you think the Divas have been changed by their experiences? In what ways do you see them responding differently to situations?

4. What does Big Mama mean when she tells Veronique that she has to "break the curse" on page 13? What other

patterns do the characters struggle with in this novel, and how do they break out of them?

5. Why does Veronique feel that her mother doesn't really love her the way she hopes her father will? Do you think she's being fair to her mother? Why or why not?

6. Veronique and Diamond are thrilled when Mrs. Silver first contacts them with an offer to help Vee find her father. But despite her excitement, Vee also knows that she will get into trouble if anyone finds out what she's up to. What is it that keeps Vee from telling anyone about her plan? Are secrets ever okay to keep? Which should you tell, and how do you know *who* to tell?

7. What clues are there that Abigail Silver is interested in more than just helping Veronique find her father? Despite her insistence that she can "spot a fake a mile away" (page 66), why doesn't Vee pick up on these clues?

8. Similarly, there are other moments throughout this novel where Veronique doesn't see the obvious. Identify these situations and explain why her "street smarts" fail her in these instances.

9. Veronique, Aaliyah, and India all discuss music that is degrading to women, arguing that "Black people need to listen to and think about what they're singing, rather than just going along because they like the beat." (page 96). Do you agree or disagree? Explain your opinion.

10. Big Mama tells Vee that she should count her blessings because she has a good life and opportunities that other girls in the neighborhood don't have. Similarly, Pastor Ford

advises Vee to "focus on the blessings, not the burdens" (page 233). What does this really mean?

11. Like most teenagers, the Divas are anxious to prove how savvy they are now that they're turning sixteen and are officially young adults. What safety rules does Veronique violate in her haste to finally find and meet her father? Identify which other characters in the novel ignore safety rules and other warning signs, and discuss the motivations that cloud their vision. Using examples from the novel, explain how misplaced confidence can interfere with good judgment.

12. What do you think the author will write about in the next and final book in the Divas series? What clues are hiding in this novel?

Enhance your Book Club Experience

1. Veronique often feels depressed about her life, especially when she compares her family and living situation to the lives of the other Divas. But Big Mama and Pastor Ford remind her to focus on the blessings in her life, rather than the burdens, so she can really see how much she has to be grateful for. Try making a list of the blessings in your life and see how it makes you feel. Practice this exercise any time you feel down about something, or even every morning as a way to set your frame of mind for the day. Share your experiences with your Book Club at your next meeting.

2. The Divas often learn the hard way that they may be young adults, but that doesn't mean they can handle everything by themselves. Sometimes they need their parents, and Pastor Ford reminds them constantly that they can and should turn to God, too. Share a story with your Book Club about a time when you thought you could handle something big on your own, and what made you finally realize that you couldn't. When do *you* turn to God for help? Do you pray on a regular basis? Why or why not?

3. Take some time to visit and browse the official Divas web-sites at www.thedivinedivas.com and www.myspace.com/divinedivaseries_2008. You can also read the author's blog at www.myspace.com/victoriachristophermurray. Come to your next Book Club meeting prepared to discuss how the internet allows authors to bring the world of their novels to life, and how this author's personal thoughts have or haven't affected your experience reading her novels.

Don't miss the next Divine Divas adventure

THE DIVAS: AALIYAH

Coming in October 2009

Turn the page for a preview of *Aaliyah*. . . .

Chapter One

I was about to have a heart attack!

And not one of those fake ones that my girl Diamond was always having. No, this was for real—the way my heart was pounding inside my chest I was gonna pass out at any moment.

When I looked over at my girls, I could tell they felt the exact same way. My best friend forever and ever, India, was standing so still, just grinning like she was in shock. And Veronique looked like she was going to faint from happiness although I wasn't sure if she was all excited about the Divine Divas or about Arjay Lennox who had stayed right by her side ever since we ran off the stage.

The only one who was standing all smug was Diamond— our self-professed leader. Yeah, Diamond was just standing with her arms folded—like this was no big deal. Like she knew all along that the Divine Divas were going to make the finals of the Glory 2 God teen talent search.

I mean, I had a lot of confidence, for sure. But no one in

the world had more confidence than Diamond. It's not that I didn't think we could sing; every single one of my girls could carry at least half a tune. But when we started this whole thing back in September, I never would've believed that we would have made it all the way to the finals. All the way to Miami—South Beach, to be exact.

And that is exactly where we were going, to Miami to compete against four other groups to shut down this whole thing and get a recording contract.

Just thinking about that made my heart start crashing again. Could this really happen? Could the Divine Divas really get a $250,000 recording contract and become big time?

Not that I was sure that this was the way I wanted it to go down. I mean, I was into winning, don't sleep. But I wasn't about to give up any part of my dreams. No way. No matter what happened with my girls and the Divine Divas, in two years, I was going to Harvard. Trust that. And, I was going to become a nuclear physicist. You could take that to the bank, too. If we won this thing, we'd just have to find a way to work it out.

"Hey, what you doing over here all by yourself?"

I looked up at Troy, one of the Three Ys Men who were our backup dancers. The way he was grinning in my face, I could tell he was as happy as we were. I guess this whole winning thing was as exciting for the guys as it was for us, even though we were the ones who were out in front.

"I'm not doing nothing." I tried to shrug Troy off, but it was hard. I could tell by the way Troy had been looking at me ever since we got to New York that he kind of liked me, but I didn't know for sure. It could've been that he just wanted to hang with me because his boys—Wiley and Arjay—had already hooked up with India and Veronique.

But it didn't matter—I liked Troy; I just didn't like him like that. Not that I wasn't into guys; I mean, Troy was major fine—don't sleep. But I had a plan for my life. And right about now, boys—even cute ones—just didn't fit in.

"So, Aaliyah, ah . . ."

"Hey, baby girl!"

Whew! I was so glad my dad came over and interrupted Troy. I could tell he was going to do something like ask me if I wanted to go out with him.

"Hey, Daddy," I said, hugging my father. He was the only male I wanted to impress right now.

"I'm so proud of you," my dad said. He looked at Troy and added, "I'm so proud of all of you. You guys were fierce."

"Oh, Daddy. Nobody says *fierce* anymore."

My dad frowned. "Nobody?"

I shook my head. "Only Diamond and Tyra."

"Well, if it's good enough for Diamond and Tyra it's good enough for me."

Troy and I laughed with my dad, but then we stopped when Roberto Hamilton, the president of Glory 2 God Productions, came into the room where we were hanging out.

"Thank you for waiting," Mr. Roberto said. "And congratulations, once again, to all of you."

As Mr. Roberto looked around the room, I did, too. Even though we were in New York, this room was filled with people from our church in Los Angeles. Besides me and my girls and the Three Ys Men and our parents (except for Veronique—Ms. Leah never came to the competitions), there was Pastor Ford and her crew. And about twenty other people from Hope Chapel packing this place.

But when everybody was as happy as we were, it didn't matter if we were standing so close it felt like we were in a nightclub or something.

"Well," Mr. Roberto's voice broke through my thoughts, "we are at the final round. How do you feel?"

He was just talking to me and my girls, but a whole bunch of people answered, "Great," "Just fine," "All right!"

Mr. Roberto laughed. "So, now that we're here, we wanted to let you know just how seriously we're taking this whole competition."

I took a deep breath.

"We're looking for the next big group."

I couldn't help but grin and my girls were cheesin', too.

"And on the G2G label, that means that we're looking for young men and women who will be able to perform at the drop of a dime, at the highest levels."

Okay, I thought. That was certainly us. I mean, we were the Divine Divas. We were . . . *fierce*. I grinned as I thought about what I'd just told my father.

"Sometimes you're going to have to perform under pressure, sometimes you're going to have to perform on short notice, you're going to have to perform with big names, all kinds of things."

It didn't take a rocket scientist to tell that Mr. Roberto was building up to something big. I guess this competition really was straight serious now.

"So because of that, we've decided to give each of the remaining groups a mentor."

Diamond was already clapping her hands like she knew who and what Mr. Roberto was talking about.

"You're going to be working with someone famous," he continued.

"Oh, my God," Diamond yelled out. She held her hand to her chest like she was going to have a heart attack.

But even though Diamond was going all the way to her over-dramatic side, I couldn't be mad at my girl. I mean, how could I when I was almost having a heart attack just a minute ago myself?

"I know who it is!" Diamond shouted out and raised her hand like we were in class or something. Now that was funny. 'Cause Diamond was in my chemistry class and she never raised her hand for nothin'!

"You think you know?" Mr. Roberto grinned.

"Uh-huh!" Diamond nodded. "It's . . . Yolanda Adams!" And then she snapped her fingers in the air like she had nailed it.

The way Mr. Roberto shook his head and Diamond pouted and frowned like she was confused made everyone laugh.

Mr. Roberto said, "I'm not going to stand here and make you guess. Let me introduce all of you to the mentor for the Divine Divas." Then he stopped like he was waiting for a drum roll.

He turned toward the door and I peeked around my dad. All kinds of people were going through my head: Beyoncé, Mariah . . . oh, oh, I know. I just loved Rhianna!

And then, she walked into the room.

"Ladies and gentleman, let me introduce . . . Zena!"

"Oh my God!"

It was Diamond screaming, but now, I was the one having a heart attack. For real, this time.

I couldn't breathe. I couldn't think. I pushed my hand against my chest 'cause I was sure my heart was going to break right through my skin.

But nothing worked.

Then my knees . . . I don't know what happened. But they felt weak.

By the time I dropped to the floor, I couldn't hear or see a thing.

Want more teen
fiction fun?
Check out these titles: